I Pucking Hate That I Love You

A novel by DL Gallie

I vowed I'd never give my heart to another hockey player again. I learned my lesson the first time. But then I met Kallen Jones and he became a huge problem.

Not only is he on my "Don't Fall in Love with A Hockey Player" list, but he's also sitting pretty high on my "I want you" list. But I can't date a puckhead again.

It doesn't matter how good looking he is with his blue eyes, lickable abs, and heart of gold. He's a hockey player and my dad is his coach. Except Kallen isn't like the others. He treats me like a princess and has me doubting my decision and breaking my vow at every turn.

Until he turns out to be just like the last puckhead I gave my heart to.

I pucking hate him but I also pucking love him...I'm so pucking screwed.

Edited by **Karen Hrdlicka**, Barren Acres Editing

Cover Designed by **R.L. Kenderson**, R.L. Cover Designs

Proofread by **Lisa Edwards** and **Margaret Neal**

Formatting and interior design by **DL Gallie**

For Tara, my wench.

1
CHELSEA

Ugh, hockey players are the biggest douches of them all, and when your dad is the head coach for the NY Crushers, one of the top teams in the league, it's hard to stay away from them. It doesn't help that I'm at Squires Tavern, the best sports bar in the city, which also happens to be the hangout for the guys on Dad's team.

Don't get me wrong, Dad's guys are great, well most of them. They look after me as if I'm their little sister. It's like I have fifteen plus big brothers protecting me, and most nights cockblocking me left, right, and center. After *him*, it's sweet but sometimes, a girl just wants a night to let out her inner minx and have wild sexy naked fun.

But no matter what happens, I will never ever give my heart to a puckhead again. Not gonna happen. Been there, done that. Got the souvenir broken heart T-shirt, and I don't need or want another one. Puck you very much, I'd rather be single than go down that road again.

"Chels," my best friend, Margot Radclyff, shouts as she places the pitcher of beer on our table between us. "There's a Hottie McHotterson at three o'clock and he's been eye-fucking the hell out of you while I was at the bar."

"You know I don't date puckheads," I vehemently retort. Of all the people in the world, you'd think my bestie would remember that.

"I'm well aware of your 'no puckhead' rule, but this guy is not a puckhead," she eagerly informs me, her voice high and laced with excitement. "I repeat, NOT a puckhead."

"How do you know?" I ask, slightly intrigued but trying not to let on that I am because Margot is like a dog with a bone when it comes to hooking me up.

"Because some chick asked him which team he played for and I quote, he said, 'I'm not a player' buuuuut as he said this to her, his eyes were locked on you."

"Interesting," I tell her.

I do the subtle twist in your chair thing and nearly fall off my stool when my eyes connect with the hottest guy I have ever seen. He has the most electric blue eyes, sandy blond hair, and a smile that goes from ear to ear. Feeling brazen because he's not a player, I throw a wink his way and turn back to Margot.

Fanning myself, I dreamily sigh. "Puck me sideways, Margot. That man is fine with a capital F." Picking up my beer, I take a sip to moisten my mouth because all the liquid in my body is currently pooled between my thighs, soaking my panties. Needing reclassification, I grab Margot's hand, drawing her attention to me. "And your one million and ten percent sure he said he didn't play?"

"Affirmative," she states matter-of-factly and nods. "But, Chels, even if he does, you NEED to take him for a ride."

"I'm not arguing with you on this, you know my mind is made up about puckheads."

"I know, I know, but that man is totally worth you letting your rule go, even just for one night. And seriously, if you were to break your self-imposed 'no puck-head rule,' it should be with him."

As I contemplate her words, the bane of my existence, Stefan Däuchmen, or Doucheman as we like to affectionately refer to him as, enters the bar. Immediately my mood dips.

My ex is the epitome of a puckhead player, douchecanoe asshole. He and I started dating when he'd been on Dad's team for two seasons. At the beginning, he was the perfect boyfriend. He was doting, caring, and before a game, he'd blow me a kiss through the plexiglass. And the sex, holy porno, Batman, it was off the charts sexy and wild...that was until I found him banging a puck bunny in our bed. I'd been out of town with Margot, helping her family with things on the farm outside Winnipeg. We got done early so I thought I'd surprise *him,* but it was me who got the surprise of all surprises. I walked into our loft apartment in Hell's Kitchen and found him pounding into said bunny, who was bent over the bed that we shared. And to add salt to the wound, I found another bunny asleep and naked on the sofa and another soaking in my bathtub.

Seems it was a swingers' party and I wasn't invited. I hightailed it out of there and raced over to Margot's place. Being the uber-awesome bestie that she is, we commiserated over ice cream, wine, and tequila. Not a very good combo the next day, but it was the best medicine to help me grieve.

My payback came when Daddy found out. He kept *him* on the bench for the last game of the season and rode his ass hard during practice. *He* being the mega douche that he is, tried to play it off as an 'accident'. What kind of fool does he take me for? You don't accidentally fall into three other women's vaginas, no one is that clumsy, and I should know because I'm the clumsiest of them all. Like seriously, Clumsy from *The Smurfs* has nothing on me.

But the kicker in the whole puck bunny saga was when he tried to blame it on me, saying I shouldn't have come home early, and if I wasn't such a lousy lay, he wouldn't have looked elsewhere.

Puck him.

That's why I will never date a puckhead again. I don't trust them and my fragile heart couldn't take another betrayal like that.

As if the gods are trying to punish me for wanting to take a chance tonight, the cause of my heartbreak and hatred for puckheads looks over to me and smirks. "Puck," I growl between clenched teeth. "Dickwank is making eye contact."

Margot knows me too well and immediately knows which dickwank I'm referring to. She spins on her chair and flips him the bird. Spinning back to face me, she stares intently at me and I know I'm about to get a talking too. "Do not let that pindicked snake take this opportunity away from you. Have a debaucherous night with that hottie and proudly do the walk of shame tomorrow, AND if Doucheman tries anything, I'll deal with him." Have I mentioned that I have the bestest friend in the history of best friends?

She heads to the restrooms and leaves me to ponder on how my night is going to end. On one hand, I'd love to hook up with the nonplaying hottie, but seeing *him* has taken the wind out of my sails. On the other hand, I have Buzz waiting at home. He won't cheat on me and I'm guaranteed an amazing orgasm with Buzz.

Decisions. Decisions.

As I sip on my beer and eat my weight in French fries, I toss her words—have a debaucherous night with that hottie and proudly do the walk of shame tomorrow—around and around, but it's hard to focus on Hottie McHotterson when I can feel *his* gaze on me.

Glancing back over my shoulder, I stare at the non-puckhead hottie again and the more I watch him, the more the idea of a night with him appeals to me. He seems so relaxed and carefree, the total opposite of a player. I think he's exactly what I need, for tonight at least.

Margot's confirmation that 'he's not a puckhead' keeps flashing in my mind, and I decide why the puck not, I'm going to take that guy for a pucking ride.

Margot returns and I finish my beer, chugging back what's left. I slam the mug down, and declare, "I'm going for it." Margot's face lights up like the arena on game day.

"That's my girl. Go have a night of debauchery with

that fine as fuck man and then when I get back from Fiji, over waffles, you can tell me all about it."

"I never kiss and tell," I tease her.

The bitch cackles like a hyena because nothing is off-limits between us, and I mean nothing. She knows without a doubt that when she's back, I will tell her all the sexy, dirty, and depraved things that I got up to when I leave here tonight with the hottie nonplayer.

2
KALLEN

"I'M NOT A PLAYER," I PAUSE AND THEN ADD, "...YET,"
I inform the brunette at the bar next to me, but my eyes
are locked on the blonde stunner across the room. As
soon as I walked in, my eyes locked onto her like a heat-
seeking missile. She has this aura about her and when she
smiles, fuck me sideways, it lights up the entire place.

Thankfully the chick next to me gets the hint I'm not
interested and moves on. She's your typical puck bunny,
desperation oozing off of her. That type of chick is one
million percent not my type. I'm more interested in your
girl-next-door type, and the babe who I have my eye on
seems exactly like that.

With a pitcher of beer in hand, I head over and join
Pearce, my new neighbor, and a few other guys from the
building: Craig, Michael, and Jaxson. I recently graduated from college, and now I officially start with the NY
Crushers as their new goalie. I cannot wait. I loved

playing during college, but I've wanted to be a Crusher since I was three years old and hit my first puck, so to have my dream finally come to fruition is pretty amazing.

Signing on that dotted line for my one point five million a year contract was better than I ever imagined. With my signing bonus, I paid off Pops and Nanna's mortgage and opened an account for my big sis to buy her own place. But the stubborn woman told me, 'I don't need a handout from my baby brother' and is refusing the money. Well, the joke's on her because that money will sit there until she's ready. I'm just as stubborn as her, I am a Jones after all.

The five of us are all new to town and from many different walks of life. Pearce is a finance guru, you wouldn't pick that considering he has tats from head to toe and wears cut-off cargos and a Henley to the office, always in varying bright colors. He and I are total opposites but as soon as we met, we clicked. Craig works at the same company as Pearce and is the executive assistant to the CEO. Michael is studying medicine at NYU and Jaxson works in PR for Life's Too Sport, the best sports PR firm in NYC. I'm considering signing with him but now that I'm friends with him, mixing friendship and business might not be such a good idea.

Stefan Däuchmen, a fellow teammate and complete and utter douche, walks in. All the girls in the bar immediately swoon over him, except my girl. Yes, I'm referring to her as mine, well, I hope like hell she'll be mine. Her indifference to him surprises me because he's the biggest player, on and off the field. Personally, I think he's the biggest douche around—his last name even alludes to that

—but now that he's my teammate, I have to smile and play nice.

"Doucheman just walked in," Pearce says.

"There go our chances of hooking up tonight," Michael adds.

"How so?" I question.

"He's the biggest manwhore around and no doubt will fuck a few puck bunnies in the bathroom before taking some skanky bunny home." He pauses. "I heard he cheated on the coach's daughter last season, that's why he was on the bench for most of the last game."

"I thought it was due to injury?" Craig adds.

"No one knows for sure, but he was seen limping around," Jaxson informs us. Him being in PR, I guess he would know. "But rumors within all come back to him cheating on the coach's daughter. That aside, he's an asshole through and through. He deserves any and all bad karma. So fucking glad I wasn't assigned him when he joined LTP." His voice is laced with hatred but when it comes to Stefan Däuchmen, most people hate him so it's warranted.

"Can't wait to get to know my new teammate better, eh," I sarcastically reply.

"Good luck with that," they all say in unison and then Michael adds, "Maybe you can hook up with his leftovers."

A shudder runs through me and I scrunch my face up. "I'll pass, thanks. I don't want anyone that wants him." Noticing the pitcher is empty, again, I grab it. "I'll get another round."

"Dude, you got the last one," Jaxson protests.

Shaking my head, I stand up. "You get the next one then." Before he can argue, I turn and walk toward the bar, taking the long way around, but I notice that she's watching Däuchmen and I deflate.

When I'm in earshot, and close enough to hear the blonde goddess and her friend chatting, I'm crushed when she says, "I'm going for it." Her friend eagerly replies, "That's my girl. Go have a night of debauchery with that fine as fuck man, and then when I get back from Fiji, over waffles, you can tell me all about it."

With less pep in my step, I continue toward the bar. I order another pitcher of beer and two tequila shots, may as well get shit-faced now. The shots are placed down and from beside me, I hear, "Is one of those for me?" I think to myself, *Why the fuck not?* When I turn my head, I'm left speechless when I see *her* standing next to me.

I stare at her open-mouthed and mute. If I don't say something soon, she's going to walk away and think I'm a dick. She turns to leave and I quickly reach out. "Sure, I'd love to have a shot off you...I mean with you."

"Maybe you can have one off me later," she coyly replies with a wink. That eye motion causes my dick to twitch and me to grin back at her.

We stare at one another, the air around us pinging with heat and desire. She reaches past me, grabs one of the glasses, and shoots it back. "Blaaargh." She winces and what comes next shocks the hell out of me. She grabs the second shot, shoots it back, grips my cheeks, and slams her mouth to mine, she transfers the liquid from her mouth to mine.

Quickly I swallow, and before she can pull away, I

grip her cheeks in my palms and keep her lips pressed with mine. My tongue slips into her mouth and in the middle of the bar we make out like teenagers.

Closing my eyes, I give myself over to her and the kiss. My cock twitches again, but this time he rises, leaving me with a semi as her tongue continues to dance with mine.

She's the first to pull back and I stare into her hazel eyes. They are glazed from either the tequila or the kiss, and going by the pink staining her cheeks and chest, I'm thinking it might be from both.

"I think that's my new favorite way to do shots," I tell her as I continue to stare at her. She was gorgeous from across the bar but up close, she's even more stunning.

She steps into my personal space; I can feel her breath on my skin. "Let's get out of here," she whispers, "and I can show you another way to do shots." She bites my earlobe and my semi is now at full mast.

"How about I buy you a drink first?"

Her eyes are on something behind me, I'm about to turn and see what she's looking at when she lifts to her tippy-toes and leans in again. She smells divine and then she whispers, "If we leave now, we can do naked shots in the privacy of your place."

That sentence abates all my fears and I feel like all my Christmases have come at once. "You had me at naked." I throw her a wink and she blushes at my response. "I just need to deliver this to my boys."

"And I need to say bye to my friend."

"Well, I'll meet you there in a sec."

"Okay." She nods and grabs the pitcher of beer on the

bar top and walks back over to her friend. I watch her ass as she walks away, biting my bottom lip to hold back the groan wanting to break free. Her ass is fine and I cannot wait to see it up close and personal as she rides me reverse cowgirl.

Turning back to the bar, I realize she took my beer. Shaking my head, I order another pitcher, and while I wait, I grin as I process what just happened. Paying for the beers—plural—I walk back over to the guys. Placing the pitcher on the table, I slap Pearce on the back. "I'm heading out." I raise my eyebrows at the boys. "Have a good night, eh?"

They hoot and holler as I walk away, but I'm stopped by Däuchmen along the way. "Jones," he snarls in way of a greeting. The sound of his voice grating on my nerves.

"Däuchmen," I tersely reply. "I was just heading out."

"I knew you were soft," he taunts, then tacks on. "I give you one season."

Ignoring the douche, I step around him and keep walking. He yells, "Pussy." But still, I don't react. I keep walking toward, hell, I don't even know her name but when my eyes land on her again, any angst from my run-in with Däuchmen disappears.

"Hello," her friend says as I reach them. "I'm Margot and you hurt my friend Chels and I'll hurt you."

"I have no plans to hurt her...unless she wants me to," I say with a wink, her cheeks darken and I find myself once again grinning.

"And who am I entrusting my best friend's care into this evening?"

"Kallen," I tell her, offering my hand.

"Nice to meet you, Kallen."

"You too, Margot." Turning to face Chelsea, I notice she's intently staring at me. "Shall we get out of here?"

She nods and stands up. Slipping her jacket on, she says goodbye to Margot and steps over to me. Lacing her fingers with mine, the two of us weave through the bar and step out onto the street. Hailing a taxi, I open the door for her and offer her to climb in first.

"Why, thank you." She curtseys, turns, and climbs into the waiting car. I can't help myself and I slap her on the ass, she squeals and giggles. It's music to my ears...and cock. Climbing in after her, we head back to my place for a night I will never forget.

3
CHELSEA

Just as we step outside, a taxi pulls up and its occupants climb out. Yes, we live in NYC but taxis are not as easy to get like they are in the movies. "Hold the door," Kallen yells and the guy, reopens it for us. "Thanks, man." The guys nod at one another just as I shudder from the chill in the air. Winter is almost upon us, but it looks like Mother Nature might be bringing the chill earlier this year.

Without batting an eyelid, Kallen pulls me into his side and guides me into our waiting chariot, slapping me on the ass which, surprising to me, causes my body to come alive. He gives the driver his address in lower Manhattan, and we settle in for the drive.

It's silent between us but it's not awkward. I keep thinking over and over that I'm a skanky hobag for leaving the bar with Kallen, but at least I know his name, making me feel less skanky ho-ish.

Out of nowhere, Kallen asks the driver to stop and he slams the brakes on. "Back in a sec," he informs me and climbs out. Turning in my seat, I watch as he races up the street and then disappears, I can't see where he went. Biting my lip, I sit here and wonder what was so important that he had to make a pit stop.

A few minutes later, he climbs back in and I glare at him with a 'what the hell' look on my face. He leans into me; I can feel his breath on my neck. My skin pebbles and my nipples pucker. He hasn't even touched me and my body is already on fire.

"I got us some tequila since you owe me a shot." He pauses, pulls back, and looks intently at me. Then he whispers, "And some condoms because after I have my shot from your delectable body," he places his palm on my jean-clad thigh and slides it up and down, "I'm going to fuck you into the wee hours of the morning. Then I'm going to have you for breakfast, and maybe lunch too." He slides his hand between my legs and ever so slowly drags it up my inner thigh, stopping just before he gets to the good bits. I groan in frustration and the pucker smirks at me. He smirks but that little lip lift is like a match to a flame, my body is a raging inferno right now. My breathing is labored. I'm tempted to straddle him right here in the back of the taxi, but with the new season around the corner, the last thing Daddy needs is a picture of me dry-humping some dude in the back of a cab. The scandal at the end of last season was enough, I won't do that to him again.

The driver pulls up in front of a building, Kallen leans forward and thrusts a few bills at him. He climbs out and bends back to offer me his hand. "Such a gentle-man," I sweetly say.

When I'm out, he pulls me into him and stares at me. Carnal desire reflects in his gaze, pretty sure mirroring mine right now. "I won't be such a gentleman once I get you upstairs and naked."

My panties literally just combusted at his words. No one has ever spoken to me like that before, and I have to say, I love the dirty talk. With *him*, sure it was hot but there was no dirty talk, so this is exhilarating and exciting.

"Well, what are we standing on the curb for then?" I tease back.

"Ab-so-fucking-lutely nothing."

He laces my fingers with his and drags me toward the entrance. The doorman opens it for us and we enter his building. "Evening, Phil," Kallen says as we walk through the lobby.

The doorman nods and smirks. He totally knows what's about to happen and surprising to me, I don't care. I can't wait to get upstairs and naked with this man.

The elevator ride is silent, except for the loud racing of my heart. I'm sure Kallen can hear it and when I glance at him in my peripheral vision, he seems calm, cool, and collected. The complete opposite of how I feel, but at least one of us is clear-headed...I think.

When the elevator dings on his floor, he takes my hand in his and we step out and walk down the hallway. I notice there's only one other door on the floor. He pulls out his keys, unlocks the door, and steps to the side, letting me pass first. He wolf whistles as I enter his apartment and I can't help but add a swing to my hips as I walk farther inside.

He comes up behind me and pulls me into him, wrapping his arms around me and hugging me, my back to his chest. My body fits into his perfectly, it's like we're two pieces of the same puzzle clicking together.

He nibbles my neck and I close my eyes and moan, dropping my head back. My nipples pebble and my clit begins to pulse. My body thrums with desire. All this and he's only nibbled me, I can only imagine what it will be like when we're naked, thrusting back and forth. The connection between us is palpable. Spinning in his arms, I drape mine over his shoulders and stare into his baby blues. "You have such beautiful eyes."

"Says the one with gorgeous eyes." His eyes roam over my face and when they land back on mine, I can feel his gaze deep in my soul. "You really are fucking stunning."

I'm not used to hearing praise so I turn and walk farther into his place. "Wow, the view from here is amazing." Before me are floor-to-ceiling windows that overlook the city, you can see twinkling city lights for miles.

"You're telling me," he says and from the tone in his voice, I don't think he's referring to the view outside.

Turning around, I lean back against the glass. "Sooo, I do believe you owe me a shot."

He stalks toward me and places the tequila and condoms on the kitchen countertop on his way past. He rests his palms on the glass behind me and cocoons me in. "I do believe that I'm to drink a shot from your delectable body." He runs his fingertip down my arm, my skin coming alive under his touch.

"I think you might be right, and you know what?"

"What?"

"Have at it." I raise my eyebrows at him, wondering where this sexy inner minx is coming from. Surprising me, he lifts me up, and on instinct, I wrap my legs around his waist. He walks over to the kitchen island and places me down on the island countertop. The granite is cool underneath but with my body temperate rising by the second, I don't feel it for long. He grabs the hem of my shirt and lifts it over my head. Leaving me in my nonsexy beige bra—thanks, Universe—my jeans and heels.

His eyes drop to my chest, he licks his lips and slides his hand around my waist, causing me to giggle. "Hmmm, someone's ticklish."

"Am not," I defensively retort, but he brushes his fingertips along my rib cage, causing me to giggle again.

"Your giggle says otherwise, but I will save that tidbit for another time because I'm a little parched right now and I need a drink."

Reaching behind my back, I unclasp and remove my bra. Dropping it to the floor, I lie back, lift my arms above my head, and stretch out on the countertop. If I thought it was cold on the ass, the granite is freezing on my back, causing my heated skin to break out in goosebumps. "Well, drink up," I purr, pushing the bottle of tequila toward him with my hip.

Without saying a word, he picks up the bottle and removes the cork lid. He tips some into my belly button and I flinch at the coolness of the liquid, but the cool is quickly replaced with warmth when he sucks and licks the tequila from my body. Then he pours a little more over my chest. He licks the alcohol from my skin, paying extra attention to my breasts and nipples. I moan in delight when he nips the tip and sucks the taut peak into his mouth.

He climbs onto the countertop with me, straddling my thighs. He stares down at me, his eyes full of hunger. "Open," he demands.

Opening my mouth, he pours some into it and before I can swallow, his mouth is covering mine. Tequila dribbles down my cheek as we kiss and make out. His tongue plunges in and out. Running my hands up the back of his neck, I scratch his scalp. We moan into each other's mouth as our tongues continue to slip and slide together.

I rake my hands down his back as far as I can and begin to bunch the material of his shirt up, sliding it over his head. Our lips only separating for the material to pass between us.

We are now both shirtless and attacking each other's mouth. He presses me down onto the counter and skims his lips down my neck, across my collarbone, and finally, reaches my breasts. He circles his tongue around my nipple, gently biting the tip again. A hiss slips through my lips at the sensation. He continues nipping down my torso, shimmying himself lower on my body until he slides off the counter and pulls me closer to the edge. He makes quick work of flipping open my jeans and sliding the denim and my panties down my legs, leaving them bunched around my ankles, my boots in the way of removing them completely.

Kallen stands up and stares down at me. Reaching out, he traces his finger up the inside of my leg, my already heated body, becomes an inferno from the intensity of his gaze and his touch. Just as he reaches the junction of my thighs, he removes his hand from my body and grabs the tequila.

He takes a swig and then pours the alcohol over my pussy. I giggle as the cool liquid trickles between my thighs. Lowering his head, he licks and drinks the tequila from my body. His tongue feels like magic and I moan.

This spurs him on and he thrusts his tongue into me repeatedly, bringing me to the brink. He pushes a finger inside and presses his thumb against my puckered hole. I tense. He reads my body, feels my hesitation, and quickly pulls his thumb back. Instead, he slides a second finger inside me, setting my body alight as my orgasm explodes. His fingers and tongue draw my orgasm from me as he laps up all of my release. Completely sated, I relax into the surface beneath me.

He lifts his head from between my thighs and stares at me. His chin glistening from my climax. Just like before, he crawls up my body and straddles me, before pressing his lips to mine. I can taste myself mixed with tequila. I moan into his kiss and against his lips, I whisper, "My turn."

"Turn for what?"

"It's my turn to lick and suck tequila off you."

4
KALLEN

Fᴜᴄᴋ ᴍᴇ, ᴛʜɪs ᴡᴏᴍᴀɴ ɪs ᴇᴠᴇʀʏᴛʜɪɴɢ ᴀɴᴅ ᴛʜᴇɴ some. I'm so glad she was referring to me when she said, "I'm going for it." For a brief moment there, I thought she was interested in douchebag Stefan. I don't get what the appeal with him is. I guess he's good-looking but as soon as he opens his mouth, and spews the shit that he does, he loses any appeal, well in my books that is. But right now, I need to stop thinking about my douchebag teammate and focus on the naked goddess beneath me.

Lifting myself off of her, I straddle her legs and stare down at her. Her cheeks are still rosy after her first orgasm of the evening. I offer her my hand; she places hers in mine and I pull her up into a sitting position.

We stare at each other for a few beats, the air around us once again sizzling with desire. She gently pushes on my chest and I realize I'm still sitting over her. I climb off her and the counter. She slips off behind me, removes her boots, and kicks her jeans and panties to the side, leaving her naked before me. My eyes roam over her body and I lick my lips. Even though I just had her, I need her again but before I can, she drops to her knees before me.

She bites her bottom lip and lifts her hands. With her eyes locked on mine, she flips my button open and lowers my fly. Sliding her hands in the waistband, she pushes the material down my legs. I help and kick them off to the side, leaving me in my black boxer briefs. My cock strains against the material, that is until she pulls them down. My cock springs free. She licks her lips and then looks up. "Do you mind if I make a mess?"

"Not at fucking all."

She smirks and winks, I don't know if I'm scared or turned on right now. Maybe both?

She reaches behind her and grabs the bottle of tequila, pulling out the cork, she offers it to me but I shake my head, eager to see what she has messily in store for me. She brings the bottle to her mouth and takes a sip. Swallowing and wincing slightly as the tart liquid slides down her throat. She licks her lips, then quickly takes another swig, this time much smaller.

Leaning forward she opens her mouth and wraps her lips around my shaft. The combination of the cool liquor and her mouth on my shaft is like nothing I've experienced before. She swallows the tequila and my cock. The tip hitting the back of her throat, she swallows again and takes my dick down her throat and begins to bob her head up and down. I thought this only happened in pornos, but fuck me sideways, this is the best blow job in the history of blow jobs.

She reaches up and begins to fondle my balls and sooner than I would have liked, they begin to tingle. "I'm gonna come," I groan, and the little minx bobs her head faster and presses that spot just underneath my balls. It sets me off and I explode down her throat with a guttural growl. She drinks every bit of my climax.

As my cock pops out of her mouth, her eyes are watering and drool drops down her chin and onto her breasts.

"That was—"

"Shit," she interrupts me. "I know I suck at giving them, but you make me want to do things that I normally wouldn't do."

"Chels, that was the best blow job I've ever had the pleasure of receiving."

Her eyes widen at my honesty. "You're just saying that because you got your dick sucked."

"Nope," I shake my head, "seriously, best head ever."

My words clearly put her at ease because she smiles. I don't get to say anything else because my brain turns to mush when Chels drops to her ass and lies back on the tiled floor. She traces her fingertip down her chest and slips it between her thighs, sliding it in and out, letting out a tiny moan. She raises her eyebrows suggestively and with her other hand, beckons me forward with her finger. Who am I to deny a naked lady pleasuring herself?

Lowering to my knees, I crawl up her body like a tiger stalking its prey. Lazily trailing kisses along the way. Covering her body with mine, I stare down at her. "You are something else, Chels."

She smiles at my comment and it lights up her face.

Lowering my head down, I cover her mouth with mine. Breaking the connection, I murmur against her lips, "I like drinking tequila with you."

"I like drinking tequila with you too...maybe we should have some more?" Before I can reply, she reaches over, grabs the bottle, and pours some onto her chest while still fingering herself. I don't know where to look, at the liquid sluicing over her breasts or at her hand between her thighs. I watch, mesmerized as the liquid splashes over her nipples, sliding down her breasts, some pools in the valley between them and the rest snakes its way down her stomach to where her hand is. Some dribbles down her sides and onto the tiles below, but I don't give a flying fuck about the sticky mess we are making. She looks innocently up at me, purses her lips, and quietly murmurs, "Oops."

"Oops indeed."

Lifting my hand, I run my fingertip through the pooled liquid between her breasts. Then I trace my finger up the side of her breast before circling her nipple. It puckers under my touch and she shivers at the contact. Leaning down, I drink the pooled tequila before licking her breast and sucking on her nipple.

She moans and arches her back, pressing her tit farther into my mouth. Raking my teeth over her nipple, I pull back and stare down at her. Once again, she's flushed and out of breath. Looking hotter than ever, her blonde hair is splayed out on the dark tiles like a halo beneath her.

Picking up the bottle, I take a swig, lean down, and kiss her. Transferring the liquid from my mouth to hers.

She hungrily kisses me back, wrapping both her arms around my neck and pulling me down on top of her. Resting my body weight on my arms—thanks, Coach, for making me do a billion planks—so I don't crush her, my tongue plunges in and out of her mouth.

"I need to be inside you," I whisper against her lips.

"I need you to be inside me too."

Reaching up to the countertop and feeling around, I grab the box of condoms. Ripping open the box, I pull out one. With my teeth, I rip the foil packet open. Her eyes watch my movements as I roll it down my shaft. Her hand has found its way back between her legs and I've never been jealous of a finger before.

Giving my dick a few tugs, we pleasure ourselves for a few moments, watching each other intently. My hand sliding up and down my shaft, her finger slipping in and out of her pussy.

"I think it's my turn," I inform her.

Shuffling between her thighs, I nudge her hand out of the way. Gripping the base of my cock, I rub the tip up and down her slit before pressing the head between her lips. Her breath hitches in her throat as I push myself inside her an inch. Pulling out, I push back in. Repeating the motion until I'm fully seated inside of her.

With my eyes locked on hers, I leisurely thrust my hips back and forth. Her eyes roll back in her head as I increase my movements. She grips and massages her breasts, pulling on her nipples. Her moans increasing in intensity.

Leaning down, I nudge her hand away with my chin and suck her nipple into my mouth. "Yessssss," she mewls, adding five extra s's to the word. "I'm close," she pants, and thank fuck for that, I am too.

Reaching between us, I circle the pad of my finger over her clit. "Puuuuuuuck," she screams as her orgasm detonates. Her body stiffens. Her back arches. She stops breathing and before she finally takes in a lungful of air, her body collapses to the tiles below, sated and content. Her reaction sets me off, and I release my climax into the condom.

Rolling off her, I lie next to her. Breathing deeply. My heart racing. Turning my head, I look over at her and find her staring at me. "I'm so glad I came home with you, that, that was..."

"Yep," I agree, panting as if I've just left a morning skate.

Removing the condom, I grab the tequila and place it on the counter before disposing of the used condom.

Walking back over to her, I kneel down next to her. Lifting my hand, I trace along her jawline with my fingertip. "Would you like to take a shower with me to freshen up, and then I can dirty you up all over again?"

"I'd like that very much." She smiles, and fuck me sideways, it hits me right in the chest. I've never had such a visceral reaction to a woman before, but there's something about Chelsea I-Don't-Know-Her-Last-Name that has me wanting more.

She stands up, and in all her naked glory, walks down the hallway toward the bedrooms, but then turns and walks back into the kitchen. I scrunch my face in confusion as I thought we were about to have a shower together. She reappears with her hands behind her back.

"I thought, before we get cleaned up, we could get a little dirtier."

"And what did you have in mind?"

From behind her back, she pulls out the bottle of tequila. "This." She winks and steps around me and toward the hallway. At the entrance, she looks over her shoulder. "You coming?"

"Hell fucking yes." I jump up and stalk over to her. Wrapping my arms around her thighs I throw her over my shoulder, slap her ass, and race down the hallway, through my bedroom and into the en suite. I place her down on the vanity.

Resting my hands on the countertop next to her, I stare into her eyes. They are a unique shade of green and in this light, I can see flecks of gold. "Sooo, what did you have in mind?"

5
CHELSEA

Leaning away from him, my back hits the mirror and I hiss at the coolness touching my heated skin. "Well," I say as I pull the lid off the bottle, "I kind of like the way you and I drink tequila together and thought..."

"You thought what?" he asks me, taking the bottle from my hands and bringing it to his lips.

"Uhh uh." I shake my head and cover his hand. "That's not how you drink it."

"Really?"

"Really, really."

"And how do I drink it?"

"From here." I push my breasts together and look down at my squished together mounds, creating my very own shot glass. Looking back up, I see nothing but hunger in his gaze that's currently locked on my boobs.

"I see," he replies. He stares up at me and with one look, my already heated body begins to sizzle. He lifts the bottle and pours the liquid into my boob cup. Surprisingly, most of the liquid stays in the makeshift cup but I can feel some of it sliding down my stomach. "Bottom's up," he says with a wink and lowers his head, sucking and drinking up the liquid. Then he licks the remaining tequila from my body.

Dropping to his knees, he parts mine farther. Lowering his head, he nuzzles my clit. "Yes," I mewl. Closing my eyes, I let all the sensations coursing through me take over as he continues to nip and suck me.

Slipping in a finger, I nearly jump off the counter when he curls his finger around, hitting my G-spot. "Yes," I coo again, massaging my breasts. I can feel my orgasm building low in my belly. The combination of him sucking my clit and rubbing that bundle of nerves inside, that no one except me has ever found before, is indescribable but it quickly dissipates and I nearly fall off the counter when I feel a pressure on my asshole. I've never done butt stuff before, it's a one-way passage and that way is out.

He quickly removes his fingers from inside me and lifts his head from between my thighs. He falls back on his feet and stares up at me. "I'm sorry," he quickly says, "I just—"

Shaking my head side to side, I stare down at him. "It's fine, I just, um, ahh, that's a one-way passage."

He nods and a silence develops between us. The sexy moment from seconds ago broken, I hate that I ruined what was building up to be a pretty epic orgasm—stupid ass being one way.

We continue to silently stare at one another until

Kallen breaks the silence. "I'll start the shower." He stands up and turns to walk toward the shower and I reach out, grabbing his wrist, halting him. He looks over his shoulder at me.

"Orrrrr, you can get back to what you were doing but just, umm, stay away from my ass."

He stares at me for a few beats and I have no clue what his answer is going to be, then he smirks at me. "Got it. No ass. One way only."

He drops back to his knees and stares intently at my va-jay-jay. "Now, where was I?"

Before I can say anything, his face is back between my thighs and his tongue is sliding between my folds. Up and down he licks, flicking over my clit with each upward stroke of his tongue. "Yesss," I pant as my orgasm begins to build once again. The impending orgasm before was edging toward strong but the interruption of assgate seems to have spurred it on somehow because out of nowhere, I clamp my thighs around his head as I reach my climax. I explode like a volcano. Screaming his name as I crash over the edge. My body convulsing as I come harder than I ever have before.

Slumping back against the mirror, I close my eyes and breathe deeply. Kallen stands up and my limp body begins to slip down. He grips my waist, holding me up. "Holy shit," I breathlessly pant. Opening my eyes, they widen when I see my juices are all over his face. "Holy shit," I rasp again, trying to catch my breath while at the same time I'm mortified for the mess I made on his face.

"Holy shit all right," he agrees, grinning from ear to

ear. "You are everything, Chels. Where have you been all my life?"

"You're not mortified that I just did that," I circle my finger around his chin and neck, "to your face?"

"No, why?"

"'Cause, I..."

"Came harder than Niagara Falls?"

"Yes, that. I'm so embarrassed." I cover my face with my hands but Kallen pulls them away and places his finger under my chin, lifting my gaze to his.

"That is nothing to be embarrassed about. I'm feeling like a fucking rock star right now."

"Really?"

"Really, really," he confirms. "Now, let's hop into the shower and see if I can make you come again."

"You're insatiable."

"Only for you, baby, only for you."

He offers me his hand and I climb off the vanity, and we hop into the shower where he does exactly that, three times. Once the water runs cold, we step out and climb into bed.

6
KALLEN

After our long sexy shower, we climb into bed and sleep together. Not sex, actual close your eyes and snore sleep. I think after the numerous orgasms, we were both shattered and can I say, lying in bed with her in my arms is a pretty awesome way to go to sleep...even if it took me a while to drift off.

Chelsea drifts off immediately, but I lie here and process the events of the last twelve hours. Here with Chels asleep, and draped over me, feels perfect in every way. I find myself grinning like the Cheshire cat. This has been the best year of my life. I scored a contract with my dream team and tonight, I hooked up with the hottest girl in the whole entire world. Where did this woman come from? I must be dreaming because shit like this doesn't happen for me, ever. My last thought before I drift off to sleep is that I'm on top of the world right now, and nothing can bring me down.

I'm pleasantly woken a few hours later with my cock sliding down Chelsea's throat. For someone who admitted last night that she wasn't a fan of giving blow jobs, she certainly excels at it.

After coming down her throat, she crawls up my body. "Good morning," she huskily purrs, and the sound of her sleep-addled voice has my cock coming to life once again, even though I just came.

"Good morning indeed," I reply. Reaching out, I cup her cheek in my palm. "Did you sleep well?"

"Like the dead. You?"

"Same...until I was woken with your delectable lips wrapped around my cock." She blushes at my comment. Running the pad of my thumb over her lip, I pull it from between her teeth. "I love that shade of pink on you, but you know what?"

"What?" she huskily replies.

"I much prefer aroused pink than embarrassed pink."

"There's a difference?"

"Let's find out."

Before she has a chance to reply, I flip her to her back and cover her mouth with mine. My tongue plunges into her mouth, and hers into mine. I haven't made out with a girl like this in forever. The moment is interrupted when my phone rings from the other room. I ignore it because this is much more important than whoever is calling me. No sooner does it stop ringing, it starts again. This happens another three times.

"Do you need to get that?"

"I want to say no, but it must be important if they keep calling."

Reluctantly, I climb off her, pull on a pair of grey sweatpants, and go in search of my phone. I find it on the island counter and I grin when I think about the fun we had on and below said counter last night.

My phone starts to ring again, snapping me back to the here and now. Picking the device up, I see it's my sister, Kendall, calling. "Heya, Big Sis."

"Kallen Matthew Jones," she bellows down the line in her I-mean-business voice. Add in the use of my full name, I know I'm in trouble, but for the life of me I cannot think what I've done wrong. "You need to call Nanna and let her know you're alive."

"Why? I spoke to Pops yesterday."

"Yes, you spoke to Pops, not Nanna."

"Ohh," I reply, rubbing the back of my neck.

"Yeah, ohh," she repeats, "and why didn't you answer when I called?"

"I was ummm, ahh, busy."

"Oh.My.God, Kal," she groans, "were you masturbating?"

"Fuck no, I'm not twelve."

"Do you have a girl there? Are you getting laid?"

"Trying," I confirm and from the grunt my sister gives me, I'm imagining her rolling her eyes at me right now.

"Why the fuck did you answer the phone then?"

"Because you repeatedly called and I thought something important had happened."

"Ohh, right. Well, go get laid and then call Nanna and let her know you're alive. And remember, if it's not on, it's not in, even though I really want to be an aunty but not because of some skanky puck bunny. We have standards in this family."

"Okay, I'm going now."

"Bye, Baby Bro."

Before I can officially say goodbye, she's hung up on me.

"Everything okay?" an angelic voice says from the hallway.

Turning my head, I smile when I see Chels has slipped into a Crushers' shirt of mine. "All good, just my sister being a pain in my ass, as usual."

"I can get going if you need me to."

Walking over to her, I slide my arms around her waist, and look down at her. "I'd very much like you to stay, I haven't had my fill of you yet."

"You're insatiable." She playfully slaps my chest. "But if you don't feed me soon, I'm going to become hangry and for the record, I haven't had my fill of you yet either, Kallen...I don't know your last name."

"Jones. Kallen Jones," I say in a suave, really bad Bond accent. Something passes over her face when I say my name but before she can say anything, I cover her mouth with mine. The kiss starts out soft but quickly turns heated when she wraps her arms around my neck, pulling me into her.

Sliding my hands down, I tap her ass and she jumps up. Walking us into the kitchen, I place her down on the countertop and pull back. "How about I make us scrambled eggs with maple bacon?"

"With coffee?"

"I think I can stretch it to include a coffee."

"You have yourself a deal. Can I help?"

I shake my head. "Nope, you're a guest. You just sit there and look pretty, but don't be too distracting because I need you to eat a hearty meal."

"Ohh yeah, and why's that?"

"Because then I'm going to eat you."

"Have at it then, Chef Jones." And just to taunt me, she leans back, resting on her hands. My shirt rides up her thighs and she spreads her legs wide. Just as I thought, she's naked under there and my cock likes the thought of her naked too. *Down boy* I internally berate myself. I focus on the task at hand because the sooner we eat, the sooner I can eat her.

Forty minutes later, we both have full tummies and are sufficiently hydrated. She places the last of the dishes into the dishwasher and turns to face me. "So, Kallen Jones." A look passes over her face as she says my name, but her next words take all my focus from her brief moment of whatever that was just now. "You promised something about eating me." She raises her eyebrows seductively and my cock is immediately at half-mast.

"That I did," I confirm, nodding. From my spot on the other side of the kitchen, my eyes travel down her body, and fuck, she looks amazing in nothing but my shirt.

Pushing off the wall, I stalk over to her. I'm a man on a mission, and that mission is to strip this woman naked and have my breakfast dessert: her. Stopping in front of her, I grip the hem of her—my—shirt and pull her toward me. "As much as I love you in this, I think it will look much better on the floor."

"Let's see." She crosses her arms, grabs the material at her sides under her armpits, and lifts it over her head. She holds it in her fingertips and drops it to the kitchen floor. She stares intently at me. The air around us thickens, much like my dick. "And?"

My eyes rake over her body. Her very naked body, and I can't help but grin. Taking a step back, I spin my finger indicating I want her to turn around. She spins around in a seductive manner and it has my cock dripping for her. "Yep, I was correct, it looks much better on the floor."

"And what are you going to do with me now?" she huskily purrs.

Stepping closer to her, I lean down and whisper, "Everything."

7

CHELSEA

AND EVERYTHING HE DOES.

Twice.

I thought our tequila session last night was hot, but the maple syrup session just now on the kitchen counter beats that hands down, however, I might need a reminder later. You know, for scientific purposes and all that, to compare which has better sexual gratification, tequila or maple syrup.

We take another shower together and even though nothing sexual happens, to begin with, it's still a sexy hot shower. Hello, hot naked guy with abs on abs and water sliding down said abs. It begins to turn heated and sexy when we start soaping each other up, cleaning off the stickiness of the maple syrup.

He tells me to turn around and then he begins to wash my hair. I've never had a partner do this before and

I have to admit, I quite like it. My moans of appreciation clearly show how much I'm enjoying it.

"You keep moaning like that, babe, and I'm going to have to get you all dirty again."

Looking over my shoulder at him, I exaggerate a moan and begin to caress my breasts. It spurs something inside of him because in the blink of an eye, he spins me around to face him, presses me back against the tile wall, lowers his mouth to mine, and kisses the life out of me.

I thought our time together last night was off the charts hot, but in the light of the day—and this shower— holy puck, man, it's like I'm living in my very own porn movie...but without the fake orgasms and cheesy music. I can quite easily see myself becoming addicted to this man.

After four more orgasms in the shower, we finally wash ourselves clean just as the water turns cold. Kallen turns off the faucets and steps out. Tucking a towel around his waist, he then grabs another fluffy towel for me and holds it out. Wrapping it around my body, he proceeds to dry me and my hair. It's totally swoony and I love every moment of it.

Climbing back into bed naked, we lie here wrapped in each other's arms. He falls asleep immediately but sleep eludes me for a bit. Eventually my eyes begin to droop, exhaustion from the multiple orgasms has finally caught up with me.

They finally stay closed and then they snap wide open. I swear my heart stops beating when I remember where I heard the name Kallen Jones before—he's Dad's new goalie.

"Pucking puck, I just slept with a puckhead," I mumble to myself.

Sliding out of bed, I pause when Kallen rolls over, but thankfully, he's out cold. Quickly I grab my clothes and slip them on. All but my panties, I cannot find them and right now all I can focus on is getting the hell out of here.

Grabbing my clutch off the kitchen island, I take one last look around his stunning apartment before I hightail it out of here.

Kallen is just another puckhead douche. He said he wasn't a player and I guess technically that's true, since he hasn't officially played his first game yet, but semantics. He lied. He's a lying puckhead. Puck him.

8
KALLEN

Before I even open my eyes, I know she's not here. I can't 'feel' her presence. I know it's weird saying that, but it's true. I've never done anything like this before, I've never picked up a chick in a bar and taken her back to my place. I'm not your typical wham-bam-thank-you-ma'am hockey player.

I've had a total of three serious girlfriends in my life and one of those was when I was ten years old. The other two didn't work out because they couldn't handle that hockey is in my blood and is my number one love. Could Chelsea be the person to take the number one spot in my heart? I don't know, but I would have liked to have had the chance to find out.

Finally, I open my eyes and yep, she's not here. Pulling on my sweatpants from earlier, I head out to the kitchen and notice her clutch is missing, but I do see that the panties I removed during our tequila session last night are still in between the stools at the island counter.

My mind drifts to her lying back on the countertop, the liquid coating her delectable body. The cute little sounds and moans she made as I sucked and licked the tequila from her skin. Fuuuuck, my dick is hard again. At least I'll have some spank bank material to get me through the foreseeable future, or until I hopefully run into her again.

Maybe I'll find her at Squires again. Seems like it's her regular hangout and since moving here, it's become mine too. There's a knock at my door and as I walk toward it, I wonder if it's Chels and she just stepped out for more tequila or something.

Swinging it open, I see Pearce standing there. "Morning."

"Morning? It's afternoon, you lazy fuck."

"Ohh," I reply, running my hand through my blond hair, "my bad. Howz it goin'?"

"Good, are we still heading out for a run...like we agreed upon last night before you so eloquently ditched us." He raises his eyebrows at me and if Chels hadn't ducked out, I'd totally be beaming right now, but my man card has been kicked in the balls.

"Ohh, shit, yeah, give me five." I usher him in. "Make yourself at home."

Racing into my bedroom, I strip out of my sweatpants, pull on some underwear, and redress. Running and no briefs makes for an uncomfortable run, my Johnson swinging side to side hurts like hell, especially after the ten miles I'm hoping to smash out today.

A few minutes later, I re-emerge in my running gear with my sneakers in hand. I look up and see Pearce holding out Chelsea's panties. "I took you more for a cotton brief kind of guy, but each to their own."

"Shut up," I snap, and snatch the offending garment from his fingers. Scrunching them up, I throw them toward the hall and quickly put my shoes on. With the laces tied, I look to Pearce. "Let's do this."

"Let's."

We head downstairs and step out onto the street. We make our way toward the Hudson and run alongside the river down to Chelsea before eventually heading back to the apartment in Hell's Kitchen.

As soon as I saw this apartment, I knew it was for me. I paid the rental deposit straight away. I hope that it will come up for sale and then it will forever be mine. Sure, at this point in my life, I don't really need a three-bedroom, three-and-a-half-bathroom place, but I fell in love with the views of the iconic Manhattan skyline and the Hudson River. The Canadian in me was stoked to see it, and I want to wake up to this every day and the view at night from the corner outdoor terrace is everything. Out there is my happy place, I imagine it's what heaven will be like. Add in the dream kitchen with oak cabinetry and chocolate red granite countertops and I just had to have it.

Walking in the door, I strip down to my briefs to cool down, perks of living alone. Heading into the kitchen, I grab a bottle of water, and head out onto the terrace. Collapsing onto the outdoor lounger, I stare out at the skyline and drink my water. I start to think about Chels and begin to wonder why she left the way she did.

We didn't get to talk much, we were, umm, otherwise occupied but from the times we did, we got along well. We are sexually compatible, and you don't have a connection like that without there also being a mental one too.

Standing up, I walk back inside and decide to have a shower before I start my meal prep for the week. I have one more week of freedom before preseason practice starts, and I will not let anything stop me from becoming the best goalie the NHL has ever had.

The next week passes by quickly and even though I returned to Squires several times, I never saw Chelsea again. I do however bear witness to Däuchmen living up to his Doucheman nickname, watching him hit on anything with tits. He really is a jerk. He is the only downside to this but from what I'm hearing, at the end of this season, Coach is going to trade him. I can handle the douche for one season.

Today is the first official practice of my rookie season playing in the NHL. As I enter the arena, I look around the lobby and take it all in. In the future, I'll enter and exit via the players' entrance, but for today, I wanted to experience it like the fans do because even though I'm a player now, I'm still a fan at heart.

This is my happy place. I was born to play hockey. I close my eyes and take a deep calming breath. Opening my eyes, I double blink because I swear I just saw

Chelsea walk through the lobby. I race farther into the arena and look around the corner, but it's empty. I must have imagined seeing her here.

She has been at the forefront of my mind for the last week. That night plays on a loop in my head and when I look in the kitchen, I'm assaulted with memories of her splayed out on my countertop with tequila, or maple syrup, dripping all over her. Shit, I've got a semi again and this isn't the time, or place. Shaking my head, I turn around and head toward the locker rooms to get changed.

Pushing open the doors, I step over the threshold and breathe in the smell—leather and hockey—there's no other way to describe it. It's intoxicating and seeps into my veins like I'm a crackhead needing my next fix. It instantly calms the nerves that were beginning to build.

Looking around the room, I take it all in. The dressing and locker rooms seem so much bigger from this point of view and then it hits me like I'm being Kron-walled—Holy shit, I'm an actual NHL player now. I have both a locker and dressing room, my own jersey, access to a state-of-the-art gym and so much more. This is a dream come true. I spy the door leading into the locker room where waiting in my cubby will be my stick, pads, gloves, and helmet. My excitement grows the longer I stand here. At the back of the dressing room and before you enter the locker room, I see the doctor and therapist's treatment rooms, the showers, and another room that right now, I have no clue as to what's in there but I'm sure it's some-thing amazing.

Walking over to my stall, I stare into it and grin when I see my official jersey, with my name on the back, hanging there. The excitement once again building when I lift my hand and trace over the letters.

"I remember that face," Anton Seaton, the Crushers' current captain says, clapping me on the back as he walks by to his stall. "That first time seeing your official jersey, it's a feeling you'll never forget."

"It's so surreal. I've dreamed of this for so long and now, now it's..."

"Yep," he replies, letting the 'p' pop. "Truth be told, I still feel the same way today. As soon as that feeling is gone, that's when it's time to hang up the skates."

As I process his words, the rest of the team begins to filter in. One-armed bro hugs are passed around. The air is electric as we all begin to change into our under gear, but that buzz dims when Däuchmen enters.

Everyone falls quiet, it's so quiet you'd hear a pin drop. The silence is broken when Coach enters the room. "Hurry up and get on the ice, ladies, your asses are mine now."

A chorus of "Yes, Coach" echoes through the room and we all hurry up. You don't want to piss the coach off, especially on the first practice.

This is it, my time to shine is finally here. I pucking love this.

9
CHELSEA

...one week later

Walking into Dad's office after receiving the frantic call just now, the first thing I notice is that he looks tired, frustrated, and concerned. My dad is none of those things, ever, so for him to look like this, something really bad must be up. He looks up and relief washes over this face when he sees me. "Pumpkin," he offers in greeting like he always does.

He walks around his desk and envelops me in a hug. "What's up, Daddy-o?"

"I need your help, Pumpkin." Two Pumpkins, hmmm, something is definitely up. "Janice had an accident earlier this week and is in the hospital. I thought I'd be fine without her, but clearly, I thought wrong. Anyway, with preseason practice having just started and the official start just around the corner, I need you to step in as my executive assistant and help your old man out."

My first reaction is, hell pucking no...times two. Working close to *him* and now, *him who I can't stop thinking about* is a recipe for disaster, and after the disaster at the end of last season I cannot do it again, to me or to Dad.

Hoping to deflect him, I focus on Janice. "Is Janice okay?"

"She will be." And much to my shitty luck, he goes straight back into the 'I need my daughter's help' part of this conversation. "I need you to step in like you used to when you were at school. You of all people know how hectic the start of a new season is, it's all hands on deck. I don't have the time or patience to train someone new." A laugh escapes me because my dad, as much as I love him, is the most impatient man on this planet, probably why his team is always on top. He doesn't tolerate shit and as soon as you're on his shit list, you're screwed.

Take what he did with Doucheman after what happened between us. If he could have fired the douche, he would have, instead he benched the asshat for most of the last game. That was the best revenge ever, even if *he* did have a slight hamstring injury. Thankfully, his contract is up at the end of this season and all going well, he'll be traded. His voice snaps me back to our conversation. "Please, Pumpkin, I need you."

Staring at my dad, I see the panic etched on his face. He raised me to help those when they need it, damn him for instilling good qualities in me. "Fine," I relent, but he and I both knew before I even walked in here today that I would because I'd do anything for my dad. "But I refuse to deal with *him*."

"Done," Dad immediately agrees. "You won't spend any time with Däuchmen, in fact, I will ban him from my office."

"Really wish you could just fire his ass."

"Me too, Pumpkin, me too, but he's a free agent after this season so, fingers crossed."

I mime crossing my fingers. "Okay, Daddy-o, what do you need me to do first?"

"I kind of need my desk back," he sheepishly says and then his eyes widen. "And what I need done like yesterday, is the processing of Jones's papers."

"Why do you need to do that?"

"Because I offered to help when some system thingy shit itself, and then Janice had her accident, and it's all turned to shit...but now that you're here, you can help your old man out."

Of course that's my first task, but I can't let on to Dad that I have seen Jones naked. Or had my tongue licking tequila off him or had his dick down my throat or that his new goalie gave me the most intense and amazing orgasms of my life. Nope, that is a secret I will take to my grave.

"Sure, no worries," I say with a smile.

"Thanks, Pumpkin. I'll get Jones to pop by after today's afternoon skate." He looks at his watch. "Which I'm now late for." He places a kiss on my head and steps around me, leaving me in his office to clean up the mess that he's created.

How he can run a successful team but keep his

office looking like this, is beyond me, clearly the game is more important than filing and organization. Looking over this desk, I laugh when I think that Janice probably hurt herself on purpose so she didn't have to deal with this and the craziness that is the start of the season.

Shaking my head, I bring up Spotify, connect it to the speaker in Dad's office, and get to it. Starship begin singing—their version—and telling me to 'don't stop believing' and as I tackle the mess that is Dad's desk, I don't believe this hell will ever end.

First task, organizing his desk. It's covered in papers, folders, and is that a, ugh, I have no idea what that even is. How he can get anything done with this mess is astounding, but I guess that's why he called me in. He can't get anything done with this mess.

Pushing his chair to the side, I grab the first pile of scouting and stat sheets, take a seat on the floor behind his desk, and start placing everything in order, ready to be filed away. I work better from the floor, even though there is a perfectly fine, albeit messy, desk at my disposal.

I'm in the middle of belting out the words to "Paparazzi" by Lady Gaga when a voice from the doorway startles me. A scream escapes my lips and I drop the papers I was holding. Looking over the desk, I scowl when I see *him* staring back at me. A shit-eating grin on his face.

"Thought I recognized that dying cat," Däuchmen taunts from the doorway.

"Puck off," I tell him, ducking back down. I blink rapidly and focus on the pile of papers that I just dropped. From under the desk, I see him step into Dad's office and walk over to the desk.

"Still not swearing I see." He leans over and stares down at me. He's trying to intimidate me but unluckily for him, I'm not giving him an ounce of my attention— even though my heart is racing, and I can feel a bead of sweat drip down between my boobs right now. "And I see you still have a killer rack." I roll my eyes at that comment. "You ready to come back to me yet, baby girl?"

Lifting my gaze, I stare up at him and glare. "Not if you were the last man on Earth," I spit at him through clenched teeth.

"You wound me, Chels." He feigns hurt and covers his heart, no chest, because that puckhead does not have a heart.

"Go find some puck bunny to accidentally sleep with, now puck off, I'm busy."

"You'll be begging to take me back one of these days."

Before I can tell him to puck off again, he turns on his heel and leaves. "I pucking hate him," I mumble to myself.

Getting back to the filing, I can't concentrate. The encounter with *him* just now is messing with my head. Closing my eyes, I swallow down the hurt that's beginning to fester once again. All these months later and it still hurts. It doesn't hurt that we aren't together, it hurts that he didn't have the respect to honor our union. "Gah, men suck."

How I could have fallen for his charm is still mind-boggling to me, but I guess we all have lapses in judgment at times. I seem to have had another one by sleeping with

Jones, even if I didn't know who he was, but I should have used better judgment. Clearly, I'm no expert when it comes to the opposite sex.

As if sensing my inner turmoil, my phone rings. Reaching up onto the desk, I feel around for it. When I pick it up, I smile when I see Margot's smiling face on the screen. I haven't spoken to her since the night I slept with Kallen and I could really do with a Margot session right now. My best friend is the bestest of best friends. I can't believe she's not here when I need her, I mean, does she really need to be there for her mom and dad's thirty-third wedding anniversary and renewal? Like seriously, who goes all out for number thirty-three? Thirty yes, hell, even thirty-five but thirty-three? Don't Mr. and Mrs. Margot know I need her?

Swiping the screen, I answer, "Hey, hey, sexy lady."

"Hey, hey, whatcha doing?"

"Filing."

"Why are you filing?"

"Helping out Dad 'cause Janice is in the hospital."

"And let me guess, in one week his office looks like a tornado went through it?"

"You got it in one...ohh and do I have news for you."

"Do tell."

"Kallen is a player—"

"That dirty fucking dog, when I get back—"

"Not that kind of player...I don't think. He's a puck-head...and Dad's new goalie."

"Shut the front door, he is not? Because I swear I overheard him saying he wasn't a player."

"I guess that night he technically wasn't 'cause practice hadn't yet started."

"How did you not know when he said his name?"

"I wasn't thinking straight, his sexiness turned me into a mush head."

"Mush head. Really?"

"Really, really."

"So it was that good, huh?"

"I was supposed to inform you over waffles when you get back, but I guess, sitting on the floor in Dad's office, surrounded by papers, is just as good." We both laugh and for the next few minutes, I fill her in.

"So, you snuck out like a skanky ho and now you're playing sexatary for his team?"

"Please do not say sexatary and refer to my dad ever again. And yes, I snuck out, wouldn't you?" I quickly continue because no, she wouldn't have snuck out. "And get this, guess who gets to process his paperwork 'cause the front office is backed up due to a system update that wiped everything?"

"No pucking way?"

"Yes, pucking way."

"Babe, I wish I was there to give you a hug, but you've got this. Just steer clear of Doucheman and you'll be grand."

"Too late for that. The puckface just left and told me that I'd be begging to take him back."

"Gah, he's such a—"

"Yep," I interrupt her because when Margot gets on a Doucheman rant, we'd be here 'til the official start of the season. If you thought I hated him, Margot hates him even more. I think she feels guilty for not airing her concerns before it all blew up in my face, but I told her, she has nothing to be sorry for. She's not the one who 'accidentally' fell into three other women's vaginas.

"Can I call you back tonight? I need to get this done and then psyche myself up for seeing Kal again."

"So, you're calling him Kal? I thought his name was Kallen? A nickname is kinda personal, don't you think?"

"Sorry, I'm... PSSCHS... losing you... PSSCHS. Talk later." And before she can prod me further, I hang up on her.

Shuffling around, I lean against the wall and sigh. She's right, I do subconsciously keep referring to him as Kal, which is kinda personal, but to be honest, I haven't stopped thinking about him all week. When Dad asked me to fill in, I got excited at the prospect of seeing him, but I can't go there. He's a player...on my dad's team and we all know how well that turned out last time. I vowed after *him* to never date a player again and I need to stick to my guns. But why do I keep falling for puckheads? Not that I've fallen for Jones, but I think I totally could.

After just one night, I was hooked but we can never be. Puck my life.

10

KALLEN

Fuck me, I thought I was fit and ready for this but I'm on the verge of dying, and that's no exaggeration. David Maxwell is a fucking sadist, plain and simple. He could have eased us into the season but nope, he went for the jugular and pushed us all, especially Däuchmen. There's definitely animosity between the two of them and I begin to wonder what that's all about. However, all is revealed when I enter the showers and overhear a conversation between two of my teammates, who are obviously not concerned about anyone overhearing them. "...seems Coach is still pissed at Däuchmen."

"Seems so but then again, that's what you get for cheating on his daughter."

Hmmmpfh, I think to myself as I step under the spray. Seems there was some truth to what Jaxson was saying.

"Also reconfirms why you never date the coach's daughter."

A chorus of "This is true" and "Yep" echoes around the showers and I too nod, that's like career suicide; just like you never date your best friend's sister...or mom. Then someone adds, "But have you seen her? She's hot as fuck and has a killer personality to go with it."

"Don't let Coach hear you say that about Chelsea," Anton adds. "After what went down, he's even more papa bear protective of her."

My eyes widen at that name and now I'm thinking about the Chels that got away. Like always when I think about her, my cock hardens and having a boner here is not the best, so I quickly think of naked fat ladies. My cock instantly deflates because no one wants to see that, but in the back of my mind—with no boner, thankfully—thoughts of my Chelsea are still there, and I wonder if I'll ever see her again.

"Might be awkward for him," Jett Jenson chortles, "'cause she's helping Coach out while Janice is in the hospital."

Silence falls as everyone processes what Jett just said. The only sound is the running water and someone's off-tune singing—my money is on James Jameson, aka JJ, because he's always singing to himself.

JJ is my brother from another mother. He and I met in junior hockey and we immediately clicked. As luck would have it, we were both drafted to the Crushers and attended the same college. We graduated together earlier this year. We are both elite prospects and officially start with the team this season. We like to hassle one another, making stupid bets, and I always remind him which one of us was drafted in the lower round. FYI, it wasn't me. This one time, we bet who could do the most bag skates before vomiting, thankfully I won because for the rest of that year, JJ had bleached blond hair with pink tips. But if anyone can pull that look off, it's him. He took it all in his stride and kept up his end of the deal, vowing to get revenge on me but to date, he's yet to secure his revenge.

Now that we're playing on the same team, I'm sure the ante will be upped but I can't wait. Bring it, JJ, bring it.

Pumping some body wash into my hand, I begin to soap up and tune them out, until I hear them mention Chelsea again. Then I start to wonder if this Chelsea is my Chelsea, not the coach's daughter Chelsea. I hope she isn't his daughter, but I also hope she is because I would love to see her again. I mean, Chelsea is a common but uncommon name, so the odds it's the same Chelsea are pretty slim, right?

"Twenty bucks says his foot will be in his mouth by the end of the week," Jett says once we're back in the locker room, changing back into our street clothes.

Everyone starts placing bets and I find myself grinning at the ease and camaraderie between everyone. The Crushers really are a great team, well, except for Douche-man, but everyone seems to be bonding over his doucheness so I guess his doucheness is handy in this instance.

Saying goodbye to the guys, I grab all the forms that someone from the front office gave me earlier this week and exit the locker room. With the paperwork in hand, I make my way upstairs to the coach's office since his executive assistant aka Chelsea—aka possibly my Chelsea—will be processing them due to some system thingy and her helping them out. I went over and over it to make sure all my I's were dotted, and my T's crossed. I'd hate for one paperwork slipup to fuck this all up for me.

The closer I get to the coach's office, the quicker my heart races. I keep wondering if the Chelsea I'm about to meet is 'my' Chelsea, and I get my answer as soon as I walk in and see a jean-clad ass bent over behind the coach's desk.

"Chelsea," I voice, not quite believing my eyes. At the sound of my voice, she stands up straight but doesn't spin around. "Chelsea," I utter her name again, and this time she slowly turns around and I come face-to-face with 'my' Chelsea.

My smile widens and my gaze wanders over her body. She's just as hot as I remember. I open my mouth to greet her properly and then I realize that I've slept with the coach's daughter. Ohh, fuckballs, I'm so pucking screwed.

11
CHELSEA

My eyes widen as soon as I hear that velvety smooth voice. The voice that has plagued my dreams and thoughts since our night together. Our night that no matter how hard I try to forget it, I just can't. The deep timbre of it vibrates through my body, lighting it up like fireworks on the Fourth. I was trying to prepare myself for this moment but no matter how many pep talks I gave myself, I was not prepared to have a reaction like this. No man has ever caused my body to come alive from just saying my name. The way his tongue wraps around the syllables does things to me that are not appropriate when we are standing in my father's office.

In any other scenario, Kallen and I could be something and I could climb him like a monkey but A. He's a puckhead. B. His coach is my dad, and C. He's a puckhead.

Puck! Puck! Puck! Puck! Puck! I internally scream.

He says my name again and I know I have no choice but to turn around and face him. Taking a deep breath, I plaster a smile on my face and spin around. I come face-to-face with the man I want but can't have.

"Hi," I whisper. "How are you?" Those three words come out huskily and sexy, totally not what I was going for, but this man does things to me.

"Good." He steps into the office and the temperature rises a billion degrees. Hell would seem like Antarctica with how hot it's just become and all he did was step over the threshold into Dad's office. "And you?"

"Good," I answer.

We silently stare at one another. It feels like it's getting hotter again and the longer we stare at one another, it feels like the room is going to combust. The arena is going to explode and it's not from the thermostat malfunctioning or a meteorite hitting the building. No, it's going to overheat and explode from the hotter than hot puckhead standing before me. The air thickens and crackles and the heat, desire, and everything else wraps around us.

His gaze is intense and I'm two point five seconds away from climbing over the desk and throwing myself at him when, thankfully, Dad arrives behind Kallen, breaking the moment or whatever the hell that just was.

Dad, being oblivious to what just silently went down between us, starts talking. "Pumpkin, this is Kallen Jones, our new goalie." He slaps Kallen on the shoulder. "Kallen, this is my daughter, Chelsea."

"We just met," I manage to squeak out.

My palms are sweaty with nerves, wondering if Dad

can tell that this hockey stud and I have seen each other naked and done wicked, wicked things to each other with a bottle of tequila and some maple syrup.

Kallen smirks at me, clearly enjoying my awkwardness. *Asshole*, I think to myself as I continue to stare at him. *Did he somehow get hotter since I saw him last?*

"Wow," Dad says, breaking the awkward silence that developed. "It looks like the filing cabinets exploded in here."

"No, Dad, that would be your desk exploded due to your lack of organization and filing skills." I shake my head at him. "I'm in the process of organizing said explosion. How did you mess this up so quickly?"

"Talent!" Dad jokes with a shrug of his shoulders. "My talent lies elsewhere."

"Clearly," I sass back at Dad.

Kallen laughs and my gaze snaps back to him. My eyes drop to the paperwork in his hand, and I say a silent *hallelujah* as I can use this mess as my escape and get him out of here sooner rather than later. "Kallen, you can pop those in the purple tray, and I'll get to them later, once I have access to Dad's desk and computer."

"What if there's an issue?" he questions, clearly wanting to spend more time with me, but that's a monumentally bad idea. He and I have already spent far too much time together, no need to add to that.

"I'll let Dad know."

"Or you could just call me?" he says, clearly enjoying me squirming.

"Or that." I stare at him, waiting to see what he's going to do next and shocking me, he places the paperwork in the tray without any further arguments. A part of me is saddened that he didn't fight harder for more time with me.

"Thanks" I hear, until he says, "Call me." He throws a cheeky wink my way and then looks to Dad. "Later, Coach."

"Good effort today, Jones, I knew you'd fit in with the guys."

"They're a great bunch."

I can't help but scoff because not all of them are great. Both Dad and Kallen look to me. "Sorry, choked on spit," I quickly lie, and then I drop down behind the desk in embarrassment and get back to the filing.

Well, I pretend to. I lean back against the drawers and close my eyes, a vision of me naked and sprawled out on Kallen's countertop flashes before my eyes. He's licking up my stomach, toward my breasts. He mashes them together and squishes his face between them. Sucking on my skin before gently biting and sucking on my nipple...quickly I open my eyes, shaking my head. I cannot be thinking sexy things like that while Dad and Kallen chat on the other side of the desk. No, I can't be thinking sexy things like that period.

Focusing on the papers before me, I get back to work and tune out Dad and Kallen. Finally, I hear the door click closed and I let out the breath I didn't realize I was holding in.

"You okay, Pumpkin?" Dad asks from above, scaring the absolute shit out of me. I scream out loud in fright because I thought I was the only one here. Looking up, I see Dad leaning over the desk, peering down at me. "You all right?"

"I thought I was alone; you scared the ever-loving crap out of me."

"Sorry, I just wanted to make sure you were okay." His voice is laced with concern. "When Jones said the team was great you disagreed, and well, we both know who isn't so great. I'm worried he'll try something with you working here now."

"I'm fine, Dad. I can handle HIM, plus I know the rest of the guys have my back."

"If my hands weren't tied, he'd be out on his ass."

"I know, Dad, and I appreciate it, but I'm a big girl. I can look after myself." *And make stupid decisions with your goalie.* "I promise that if he tries anything, I'll let you know, but surely he's not that stupid."

"It's Stefan, Pumpkin, he's the definition of stupid. Maybe I should let Kallen know to steer clear of him."

Shaking my head, I stand up, walk around the desk, and over to him. He spins around and leans against the filing cabinets. I mimic his pose and he pulls me into his side for a sideways dad hug. "I'm fine, Dad, and I can handle *him*. You don't need to create any more angst in the team because of me, last season was it. It's a new season and we need to focus on winning the Cup. Yes, Kallen is new so he's not aware of what went down, but I assure you, I'm okay and I will never be with another puckhead again."

"How did I get so lucky to have such an amazing daughter?"

"'Cause she has two amazing parents guiding her."

Even though right now your amazing daughter is a big fat liar, liar pants on fire, because I got down and dirty with your new goalie just recently. But that's not going to happen again so I'm not lying, just omitting the truth. I mean, it's not like I'll see him all that much. He'll be on the ice, and I'll be locked away in Dad's office. Easy, right?

12
KALLEN

So, she IS 'my' Chelsea but from the interaction just now, she wants nothing to do with me. Rounding the corner, I run into the last person I want to see.

"Stay away from her," Däuchmen warns me.

"What?" I snap, surely he doesn't know about Chels and me.

"Chelsea, stay away from her."

"Oooookay," I drawl out the o's. "I wasn't aware you were dating—"

"She's mine, just remember that."

"You wish she was still yours," Anton snaps at him, joining us. "You did enough damage to that girl and if you want to stay on this team, it's YOU who needs to stay away from her."

"Just because you're the captain, doesn't mean I need to listen to you off the ice. If I want her, I'll have her."

"Like you stand a chance with her after what you did to her last season," Anton growls at him, I have never seen him angry like this before.

"Fuck you, Seaton," he snaps and turns his attention to me. "Just remember what I said, Jones. Stay the fuck away."

He turns and walks away from us. Leaving me confused and pissed off. He slams the door to the locker room, the handle banging against the wall, the sound echoing through the hallway.

"He's—"

"A douche," Anton interrupts, "his last name is totally on point."

"Definitely. What's with him and the coach's daughter?" I voice the question that's been running through my head since I realized that my Chelsea is the Chelsea that the guys were referring to in the showers earlier.

"He screwed her over in the worst possible way last season. Avenging his daughter, Coach benched him during our last game. Doucheman," he growls his name, "thinks it's all Coach's fault that we lost because he didn't get much ice time. Newsflash, Doucheman is not that good of a player, and we would have lost even with him having more ice time. The Bears were a far superior team last year but this year, they're going down because word on the street is that the Crushers have a new goalie and he's up there with the greats."

Hearing him refer to me like that is amazing because Anton Seaton is one of the greats. He's Gretzky great, so to hear that from him, I'm speechless.

"Well, I hear that it's because the team has a great captain."

"And don't you forget it." He winks at me. "But seriously, man, stoked to have you on the team."

With that, he slaps me on the back and walks toward the exit, leaving me standing here with a goofy grin on my face.

A door opens down the hallway and when I turn my head, I smile when I see Chelsea. She looks up and our gaze connects, her steps falter, and we silently stare at one another. Her face drops and a few seconds later, I'm shoved from behind. Stumbling, I manage to not fall on my ass. "Stay. The. Fuck. Away," Doucheman growls as he storms past me. He blows Chelsea a kiss and walks out the front doors.

Staring at his retreating form, I didn't even notice Chelsea walk over to me until I feel her hand on my arm. "Are you okay?" she timidly asks.

Nodding, I stare over at her and smile. She squeezes my arm and as if she realized what she just did, she quickly pulls her hand back. We say each other's name at the same time, but I quickly tack on, "You first."

She nods and bites her bottom lip. "Look, Kallen, I... we...what happened between us can't happen again. You're a puckhead and my dad is your coach."

"So? What's my profession or your dad got to do with anything with us?"

"It has everything to do with us." She sighs in frustration. "You said you weren't a player."

"We never discussed my profession."

"Margot heard you at the bar say you weren't a player."

"Well, Margot heard wrong and who gives a puck if I'm a player?"

She smiles and laughs. "You said puck."

"Yeah and?"

"I do that instead of swearing too."

"Then it's fate that we should be together."

"Pretty sure that's not how fate works but I'm sorry, I can't date another player."

"Because of Douche...I mean Däuchmen?"

Her eyes widen. "You know about that?"

"Not the specifics, but I'm guessing he pucked you over and lives up to the Doucheman moniker."

Again, she laughs. "That's my nickname for him too."

"I think it's everyone's nickname for him. Really suits the royal doucheness that he is."

She laughs again and it's music to my ears. "You have a beautiful laugh."

"You've been hit in the head too many times with a puck if you think my laugh is beautiful, but I appreciate the compliment."

"Just stating the truth." I pause and wonder if I should say what I want to say next and I decide to just go for it. "It's a beautiful laugh for a beautiful woman. Chels, I haven't stopped thinking about—"

She presses her finger to my lips and when the pad of her finger touches me, a jolt of electricity sparks between us. "Don't, Kallen. Just don't. It was one night and that's all it will be."

"Why?" I ask against her finger.

"Because you're—"

"A hockey player and your dad is my coach. Got it but, Chels." I take a step closer to her and cup her cheek in my palm. "I don't give a flying puck that your dad is my coach. I like you and I'm pretty sure you like me too. I'm a patient man, Chels, and I'll wait for you because someone like you is worth waiting for."

Leaning down, I place a kiss on her cheek. Turning on my heel, I walk toward the exit. With my hand on the door handle, I look over my shoulder and see her staring at me. "I'll be seeing you, Chelsea Maxwell."

Pushing the door open, I step out into the crisp New York October air and take a deep breath before heading to my car. I can still feel her gaze on me as I walk through the parking garage. Glancing over my shoulder again, I notice she's still watching me, and I can't help but grin. I know that she wants me just as much as I want her, I just need to find a way to win her over. Game on, Chels, game on.

13

CHELSEA

Standing here with my cheek buzzing from where he just kissed it, I watch him walk away from me. "I'm so pucking screwed," I mumble to myself. "Why, ohh pucking why, are you a puckhead?"

Shaking my head, I turn around and make my way back to Dad's office. Stepping over the threshold, I close the door behind me and flip the lock. Leaning against it, I slide down to my butt, pull my knees up, and rest my head on them. Closing my eyes, an image of a smiling Kallen appears before me, but it quickly morphs into a smarmy, smiling image of *him*. Why after all this time is he still haunting my thoughts? I'm not even upset over it anymore, but since realizing that Kallen was a puckhead and on Dad's team, I'm back to square one with him taunting me again. And my run-in earlier only confirms how much of a douche he really is.

This is why I don't date puckheads. There's too much

at stake, especially for Dad, and I cannot do that to him again. I nearly ruined his team once by dating one of his players, I will not do it again...no matter how pucking hot he is.

Pulling on my big girl panties, I stand up and my eyes land on the paperwork that Kallen left. I know processing that needs to take priority, but my big girl panties are currently more like a skimpy pair of cheeky briefs. So, I ignore the glowing white stack of papers waving their sparkly jazz hands at me and focus on the filing I was working on earlier.

Bringing up Spotify, I click on my daily mix and "I Gotta Feeling" by Black Eyed Peas blares through the sound system in Dad's office and I get to it...but each time I walk over to the filing cabinets, that paperwork catches my eye. "Ugh," I groan. Slamming the draw shut, I grab the offending papers and walk over to the desk.

Booting up the iMac, I open the documents I need ready to input all the data but when I look at the sparkly jazz hands waving paperwork, I shake my head. Kallen Jones may be a sexy as puck puckhead but his handwriting is atrocious. I cannot read a word of his chicken scratch. "Dammit, I'm going to have to call him."

"Call who?" Dad says. I was so engrossed in the messy handwriting that I didn't even hear him open the door. The door, which was locked, so clearly, the lock doesn't work.

"Jones, his handwriting is worse than yours. I cannot read it."

"Surely it's not that bad."

Giving Dad 'the look,' I pick up the first page and turn it to face him.

Dad groans. "Thankfully good handwriting isn't a requirement to play hockey, otherwise Jones would be pucked." I laugh at that. "Don't call him back now, I'll tell him to pop by after the morning skate."

"Thanks, Dad." And I really mean it because the less time I need to spend talking to him the better. I think Margot and I need a night out. I need to drink away all the memories of Kallen-Pucking-Jones but my best friend is away until the weekend so I guess it will be Ben & Jerry's and whatever wine is on special to keep me occupied tonight.

Deciding I've had enough for today, I file the last few papers that I've sorted. I can tackle the rest tomorrow, along with processing Kal's paperwork, but thankfully with a desk between us I should be safe, right?

14
CHELSEA

The next day I'm nervous and on edge. Every time there's a knock on the door, I crap my pants or I jump in fright. I've managed to get Dad's desk cleared and his appointments in order. How he functions on a daily basis I will never know, but I guess with Mom guiding him at home and Janice here at work, he never has to worry.

Speaking of Janice, she's now at home and resting, but it looks like she'll be out of action for a few more weeks. Not the news I wanted to hear, but Janice's health is more important than me trying to hide from *him* and *him*.

Just after lunch, the knock I was dreading comes. I could feel him before I even heard the rap rap of his knuckles on the door. Looking up, my breath hitches when my eyes land on him. He's in sweatpants and a Crushers' long-sleeve T-shirt. The material stretches over his chest and wraps around his muscular arms, high-lighting each and every muscle in his upper body. *Puck me, this man is fine.*

"Hi," I finally manage to say, after not so subtly checking him out, and going by the smirk on his face he knows exactly what I just did.

"Hey," he says, stepping into the office, closing the door behind him.

Swallowing deeply, I watch as he walks over to the desk and takes a seat across from me.

"So, you need me?"

Yes, I need you. Naked and... Stop it, Chelsea Maxwell, you will not lust after the hockey player. YOU WILL NOT.

"Your handwriting is worse than Dad's."

"I'll take that as a compliment," he cheekily throws at me.

"It wasn't a compliment. It's worse than a first grader."

"Thank you, that's a step up. My sister says kinder-gartener so I'll take first grader."

Shaking my head, I grab the paperwork in question. "So, I'm going to have to fill this out manually and then input it as we need hard copies as well as electronic ones."

"Why in this day and age do we need hard copies?"

"Beats me, I don't make the rules, I'm just following what the front office has asked." *And silently I yell at them for making me do this and being in close proximity to Kallen-Pucking-Jones.*

"I can definitely see you as a rule follower."

"And you're a rule breaker," I throw back at him.

Leaning forward in my chair, I cross my arms, resting my elbows on the edge of the desk. Kallen's eyes drop to my chest. Looking down, I realize the buttons on my sleeveless top have popped open and right now, he has a full view of my pale pink and black *Victoria's Secret* bra and cleavage—cleavage which thanks to my bra is on point today. "Shit!" Spinning the chair around, I redo the buttons. Once the girls are safely hidden from view, I turn back around to a grinning Kallen.

"It's nothing I haven't seen...or tasted before." My eyes widen at his comment. "I know you want me, Chels," he says, his eyes boring into me. Am I that transparent? Or can he feel what I feel whenever he's around? He's not being cocky right now, he's stating facts. Facts that I cannot deny but I just can't. He's a hockey player... on my dad's team and I can't do that again.

"No, I don't," I repeat again, but we both know I'm full of shit.

"Yeah, Chels, you do."

"You lied," I timidly say.

"How did I lie?"

"You said you weren't a player."

"I thought you meant in the sleep around hump-and-dump way."

"I would have preferred that."

"What do you have against players?"

"Aside from the fact that my dad is your coach." Shaking my head, I swallow down the lump in the back of my throat. "It doesn't matter."

"It matters to me because I like you, Chels. I really

like you and I think deep down you like me too, but for some unknown reason it scares you to take a chance with me. Why?"

Shaking my head, I state, "It doesn't matter why, I...I just can't. I can't do that to myself again." And I hate that *he* still has this hold on me because I'm pretty sure that if I didn't have a past with puckheads, I would jump with both feet into something with Kallen, but I can't open my heart up to that again. My heart wouldn't survive a second break.

"Do what?" he pleads. I know I should tell him but it's too hard, and really, it doesn't matter. At the end of the day, he's a player and after *him,* I said I'd never date a player again and I need to hold true to myself. I need to protect me and my heart.

"I'm sorry, Kallen, it's never going to happen."

"Never say never," he states matter-of-factly. "Chelsea, you and I, we had a connection that night and that's not something to walk or sneak away from."

"We can't," I quietly whisper.

"Because of Däuchmen?"

"You already know everything, don't you?" I ask. I should have known the specifics would come out, but there was a part of me that was hoping it would have been brushed away.

He nods. "Yeah, and I can unequivocally say, he's a douche for walking away from you. If you were mine..."

"If I was yours, what?" I breathlessly ask, and he notices the hitch in both my breathing and voice.

He stares across the desk at me, his gaze is heated and carnal, reminding me of the night we spent together. My panties dampen when I realize that I can feel him deep in my soul. "If you were mine, Chels, I would never let you go."

"You...you can't say things like that, Kallen."

"Well, I just did." We both fall silent, staring at one another. "Let's get the paperwork done so I can take you out for coffee."

"Paperwork, yes. Coffee, no."

"We'll see."

For the next thirty minutes, we refill out all of his paperwork and thankfully he doesn't need a visa—thank you US/Canadian government agreement—so that's one less hassle and we can wrap up our time together quickly.

"Looks like we are all done, Mr. Jones."

"Why thank you, Ms. Maxwell." We stare at one another, and the temperature starts to rise. "So, how about that coffee?"

"If I remember correctly, I said yes to the paperwork. No to the coffee."

"All I heard was yes."

Shaking my head, I can't help my grin at his cockiness.

"Is that a smile I see, Ms. Maxwell?"

"Maybe...but the answer to coffee is still no."

"Why?"

"Because."

"Because, really? That's all you've got."

"Yeppp," I reply, letting the 'p' pop. "Plus, I have somewhere I need to be."

"Are you brushing me off? Or do you really have somewhere to be?"

Shrugging my shoulders at him, I begin to shut down the computer. I grab the recently completed legible paperwork and place it straight in an internal envelope to send over to the front office. Of course, I need to bend down to place it away and even with my back toward him, I can feel his gaze roaming over me.

Standing back up, I turn around and lean against the filing cabinets and stare over at the hotter than hot puck-head. He opens his mouth and I raise my hand, halting him. "I said no, Jones, and no means no."

"Duly noted, but you need to know, I don't give up easily. You will be mine. Mark my word. I don't give up easily and I'm not walking away without a fight because you, Chelsea Maxwell, you are worth it. You are worth everything in the world." The look of determination on his face crushes me because they are the kind of words every girl dreams about, but I need to be strong.

He walks over to me and places a quick kiss on my cheek. We stare at one another, and I want more than anything to pull him into me and kiss him, but I can't.

"Goodbye, Kallen Jones," I quietly whisper, my voice wavering.

"Goodbye, Chelsea Maxwell." With that, he exits Dad's office, leaving me confused about what I really want and wondering if I actually can stay away from him.

Putting one foot in front of the other, I walk over to the door and poke my head out into the hallway. I watch him walk away from me. I'm glad I stuck to my guns but at the same time, a part of me wonders if I've made a huge mistake...I pucking hate this.

15

KALLEN

Walking away from Chelsea just now was hard. I know I need to give her space, but what she needs to realize is that I meant every word I just said. She's worth fighting and waiting for. I need to give her time and space to get used to the idea of us, but I won't be staying away completely.

How Doucheman could have cheated on her is beyond me. She is the epitome of the perfect woman and her tits, fuck, I forgot how phenomenal they were. Encased in that sexy as sin bra only amplified how amazing her rack is. I'm a total boob man, and her boobs are one of the many reasons I like her. How I didn't get a boner when I saw them was beyond me, guess my dick was looking out for me for once.

Climbing into my Supra—yes, the same car from *Fast and Furious* but mine is phantom gray and not burnt orange—I start the engine and rev it. The sound echoes and vibrates through the car. Backing out of my spot, I exit the underground garage and head out into the bumper-to-bumper NYC traffic. I thought traffic in Vancouver was crazy but it's nothing compared to this.

Pulling into my parking spot, I climb out and when I enter the elevator, it stops at the lobby. It feels like everyone in the building enters and we stop multiple times before finally arriving on my floor.

Walking down the hallway, I unlock the door and enter. No sooner does it close and there's a knock. Opening it, I see a grinning Pearce. "Howz it goin'?"

"Your Canadian is showing, man," he teases me. "A smile and hey, how you doing will suffice."

"Did you just Joey me?"

"No, I greeted you hello plus, Joey says 'how you doin' not 'how you do-ING.'" He places emphasis on the 'ing'.

"Whatever. What's up?"

"Was stopping by to see if you wanted to join me for a run?"

"Not today, I'm beat after today's practice."

"Sounds like you need a run to increase your stamina...no wonder that chick ducked out on you."

Flipping him the bird, I turn my back on him and he follows me into the apartment. Dumping my bag beside the island, I grab a water from the fridge and make my way out onto the balcony.

Leaning on the rail, I look over the city. "What's on your mind? You're a million miles away."

"Chelsea."

"Dude, you need to get over her. Chances of running into her are eight million to one."

"Ding. Ding. Ding. I win."

"You saw her again?"

"Yep, twice now. Turns out, she's the coach's daughter."

"No shit."

"Yes shit, and just to add salt to the wound, she's his assistant at the moment."

"No shit."

"Will you stop saying no shit?"

"I'm kinda speechless. How did you not know she was the coach's daughter?"

"Didn't really stalk my coach."

"So how did the seeing of her go?"

"She's just as gorgeous as I remember but wants nothing to do with me."

"Ouch."

"Yeah, ouch, but I'm gonna get her to give in. She's..."

"She's what?"

"Everything."

"You feel she's 'the one'," he air quotes the one, "after banging for one night?"

"I can't explain it, man. I just know, eh? Like, it's this sixth sense that she is."

"They do say when you know, you know."

"Yeah, now I just need to get her on the same page as me. She's not a fan of puckheads."

"How so?"

"Doucheman is her ex. He screwed her over, literally—"

"So THAT's why he sat out the game."

"Yep. Coach couldn't fire him, so he benched him instead. Personally, I think that's worse than being fired, but anyway, 'cause of him, she'll never date a puckhead again."

"Then why did she sleep with you?"

"Technically, I wasn't a player when we hooked up."

"So, you snuck one in on the sly."

"It was more than one," I cockily tell him with a wink.

He shakes his head. "So, what are you going to do?"

"Win over the girl," I honestly tell him, that's all I want. I want Chelsea, like I want the Crushers to win the Cup.

"How you going to do that?"

"No clue. Any ideas?"

"You're on your own there. Maybe you need a woman's perspective. How about your sister?"

"She's as unlucky in love as I am. I'm pretty sure her current beau, Chad, is gay but neither he, nor she, can see it."

"Is he a douche? 'Cause all the Chads I know are douches."

"He's all right. Treats K well, but I think he'd rather be dating me than her."

"Someone's high on themselves."

"Just stating facts but if he hurts my sister, I'll hurt him."

"You're a good big brother."

"Younger, she's older than me."

"Whatevs, you're a good guy, Kallen, and I'm sure Chelsea will see it too and give you a chance."

"I hope you're right, man, I hope you're right."

16

CHELSEA

HE POPS IN ONCE A DAY JUST TO SAY HELLO, I MEAN taunt me and remind me that I'll be his again, but in actual fact, he's reminding me of what a total jackass he is. I know if I tell Dad, he'll try benching *him* again but I'm a grown woman, I don't need my daddy fighting my battles for me. Instead, I'm playing the silent treatment card, see I'm totally mature. Margot thinks I need to junk punch him but then I'd have to touch him and get a tetanus booster, so silence it is.

Margot arrives home today, and we are going to meet up at Squires for beers, wings, and a much needed face-to-face catchup. She is NEVER allowed to leave me again. I really could have done with a beer and wing catchup a week ago. Sure, we drank wine and ate nachos via FaceTime, but it's just not the same as in person.

Thankfully, Dad has arranged an evening skate for the team today so there's no chance that Kallen or *him* will be there. I can have uninterrupted girl time with my bestie.

Locking up Dad's office I pause when I feel him nearby. I don't know what it is, but I get this sixth sense when he's close by. Margot thinks it's fate and we're meant to be but there's one, well three, problems in her theory. One, he's a puckhead. Two, my dad is his coach, and three, I will never ever ever date or fall in love with a puckhead again.

"How's it going, Chels?" His deep voice vibrates through my body.

Turning around, I smile. "Good thanks, and you?"

"My day just got better."

"And why's that?"

"Because I saw you." Before I can reply, he winks, spins on his heel, and heads off to training. I stand here and watch or perv—whatever—on him as he walks away. My eyes home in on his sexier than puck ass, that's encased in dark sweats. Most women go gaga for gray sweats but for me, I don't care on the color, sweats are hot, period! Plus, it's what's under the cotton material that I care about and luckily for me, I have seen said ass in all its naked, beautiful pucking glory. Shit, now I'm thinking about that night, again.

"You all done for the day, Pumpkin?" The sound of Dad's voice startles me, and I scream in fright, dropping all the mail I had in my hands.

"You trying to kill me, Dad?"

Dad drops down and picks up the mail. "Sorry, Pumpkin, I didn't mean to scare you. Your head was in the clouds."

Yeah, thinking dirty things about your new goalie's naked, delectable ass. "Sorry, just making sure I had everything before I head out. Margot is back today and we're meeting up at Squires."

"Say hello to my adopted daughter."

"Will do, Daddy-o. Do you need anything else before I go?"

"No, it's all good, Pumpkin." He walks over, pulls me into his side, and places a kiss on my head just like he always does. "You really are a godsend. I'd be lost without you right now."

"You'd survive. Just. But you'd survive."

"You are a cheeky monkey, just like your mother. Speaking of her, she wanted me to remind you about the annual preseason team dinner this Friday. Since you're working for me, she thinks you should be there too."

"Is that just an excuse for her to see me?"

"Probably," he says with a shrug.

"I'll call her and arrange something before then because I don't really need to be there. I'm not really a part of the team."

"Anyone who works for the Crushers is part of the team, you know that. We're one big family. From the cleaners to the laundry to the—"

"I get it, Dad, one big happy family." *Complete with annoying members who you just wish would go away.*

"We sure are. Now, call your mother and see if she needs a hand with it. I'm so proud of you, Pumpkin."

"How are you proud of me? I'm a college dropout who has no clue what she wants to do in life."

"You may be a college dropout, who has no clue what

she wants to do in life, but right now, you are the executive assistant to the Crushers' head coach, and I would be lost without you. The season would have started off on a shit note had you not stepped in. You don't know how appreciative I am of you doing this."

"Dad, it's nothing, really."

"It's everything to me...and the team."

Hearing that from him makes me feel all warm and fuzzy. When my life imploded, I dropped out of Columbia, and I've been coasting by ever since. Taking temp job after temp job. In a way, *him* screwing me over helped me realize that I wasn't doing what I was meant to be doing with my life, so I dropped out. I was only doing art anyway, like really, what could I do with an art degree?

"Dad, you know I'd do anything for you, and to be honest, I've had fun doing this and, surprisingly, you're not that hard to work for."

"Maybe you can take over when Janice retires?"

"Let's not get ahead of ourselves. We might hate each other after this."

"If I haven't killed you already, Pumpkin, I think we'll survive this. I mean the hormonal teenager years have passed. It's not like you're planning on sneaking out and hooking up with my players in the showers."

"No!" I refute quickly, while internally I'm thinking, *Oops, been there. Done that. Got the sexy tequila/maple syrup-soaked shirt and memories.* "I told you, no more puckheads."

"You okay, Pumpkin, you got flushed all of a sudden?"

"I'm fine, Dad, just embarrassed at the compliment from you just now." *That was a good cover, Chels.* "I need to get to the front office and get this all sent off. I'll see you tomorrow morning."

"Have fun tonight and don't forget to call your mother."

"Will do, Dad. Have a good session and give *him* hell."

"Always." He winks, then turns and walks toward the rink. Leaving me standing here wondering how I will get out of this dinner on Friday night.

"I missed you," I greet Margot when she finally arrives after her flight being delayed for three hours. Throwing my arms around her, I hug the life out of my sister from another mister. She is my ride or die and I've missed her so much while she's been away.

"I missed you too." She sits across from me and picks up my beer and takes a big sip.

"You good?"

"Yep, you know I hate flying."

"Your fear of flying is based on a dumb movie."

"I will have you know, *Final Destination* is NOT a dumb movie, and that plane crash at the beginning could totally happen in real life AAAAAND there's also *Con Air, Snakes on a Plane* and finally, *Red Eye*—Cillian Murphy is totally hot by the way."

"Yes, he is hot, but your fear is totally weird. Fear of flying aside, how was it?"

"Beautiful, absolutely beautiful, Chels. I wish you could have been there. Fiji is the epitome of gorgeous, and the men," she fans herself, "we definitely need a girls' trip there."

"Sounds like a plan," I happily agree, because then maybe after hooking up with an island non-puckhead hottie, I'll forget all about a certain Canadian puckhead.

"Enough about me, tell me alllllll about your puck-head woes."

I fill her in on the last week, going into all the sexy details that I didn't over text or FaceTime while she was away.

"That's quite the dilemma that you have there."

"Any suggestions on how to fix this?"

"Become a nun and move to Tibet."

"Why Tibet?"

"Isn't that like the holy grail for nuns?"

"That's monks, I'd think a nun's holy grail would be The Vatican."

"In Rome?"

"Technically no, The Vatican is located in Vatican City and is encircled by a two-mile border with Italy. Vatican City is an independent city-state that covers just over one hundred acres, making it one-eighth the size of New York's Central Park."

"You are such a geek knowing that," she teases me.

"No, I just paid attention when we went to Italy with school in senior year."

"That was such a great trip."

"For someone who hates flying, you sure are a jet-setter."

"Bite me." She sticks out her tongue. "Right. So, moving to Vatican City and becoming a nun is off the table. You want to know what I really think?"

"Yes." *No, because I know she is going to tell me to go for it.*

"I think you should go for it with Kallen. Puck *him*. *He* does not control your life and dictate who you screw. Besides, do you really want to give all of that sexy schmexy up? 'Cause from what you've told me, he pucks like a porn star, which is perfect for you and your va-jay-jay."

"You really have no filter, do you?"

"When it comes to porn worthy sexy schmexy, no pucking way. I say ride that Canadian for all he's worth and you never know, he might be 'the one' you've been searching for."

Margot heads to the bar to order another pitcher of Millers and our first order of wings, leaving me to think over her words. Can I give him a chance? Kallen is nothing like *him,* but can I open my heart up to a puck-head again?

And as if fate is taunting me, the puckheads and team walk into Squires. *Puck my life, just one night, is that too much to ask for?*

Like a heat-seeking missile, our gaze connects, and something passes between us. Something that has me making a decision right here and now, I decide that I'm going to take a chance and go for it. Upgrading my skimpy pair of cheeky briefs to my big girl panties, I take a risk and smile at him, giving him sexy, flirty eyes in hopes that he'll come over to me. Either I suck at the sexy dirty eyes or I'm misreading everything because to my dismay, he follows the rest of the team to the other side of Squires. Leaving me once again flummoxed by a puckhead.

17

KALLEN

Walking into Squires, my eyes immediately land on Chelsea and if I wasn't here with the team for a bonding session, I would head over and chat. Something in her gaze just now gives me hope that she's warming up to me, but when I look back over to her after taking my seat next to JJ, I notice that she looks angry and pissed off all of a sudden.

"What's going on between you two?" JJ questions, nudging me in the shoulder and head nodding toward Chels.

"Nothing," *Yet,* I silently add.

"Nothing my ass. Blind Freddie can feel the tension between you two."

Looking over at him, I decide I can tell him what happened. Of all the guys on the team, he and I are the closest since we already knew each other before we joined the team. "Before I started with the Crushers, I had a one-night stand with this girl and—"

"No way, you fucked the coach's daughter?"

"Shhhh, keep your voice down." I look around but everyone seems to be engrossed in the baseball playoff game currently playing on the big screen. "I didn't know she was his daughter and we, kinda, umm, ahh, didn't do much talking, if you know what I mean."

"You dirty dog you. And let me guess, when she found out she freaked out and left."

"Well, she snuck out while I was sleeping."

"You got fucked and chucked by the coach's daughter, this just keeps getting better and better," he teases, slapping the table and throwing his head back laughing.

"Fuck you, asshole." I punch him in the arm playfully.

"I'm just teasing. So, what's the issue?"

"She doesn't want me. Tells me she can't again, blah, blah, blah."

"Well, after Doucheman fucked her over how he did, I can see why she'd be hesitant but, dude, even I can feel the sexual tension between you two and I'm not even remotely in touch with my feminine side."

"I don't know what to do. I really like her."

"So go over there and tell her. Make her feel wanted and appreciated and whatever you do, if you get a chance with her, don't sleep with three puck bunnies."

"Dude, if I get a shot with her, I won't be fucking it up."

"Well, what are you waiting for?"

"We're meant to be here for team bonding and I'm

pretty sure Coach didn't mean me bonding with his daughter."

"I'll cover for you, just go take a piss or something. Work your magic with her and then come back with beer and cheese sticks."

"Is that your way of telling me you want beer and cheese sticks?"

"Yep, now chop-chop, lover boy. I need beer and gooey cheese and you." He swirls his finger in my face. "You need to get the girl."

Shaking my head, I head toward the bar and order two pitchers of Miller and an order of cheese sticks for JJ. With the pitchers in hand, I walk back to the team and place them down. Garnering myself a round of backslaps and cheers from the guys when I return with the glasses.

Everyone is having a good time, except for Douche-man. He looks at me with contempt and sneers, "Look at the beer bitch doing his stuff, show us ya tits, Canada Boy."

"Shut your mouth, Däuchmen," Anton berates him. "We only tolerate you because we have to. If you don't want to be here and be a part of this team, there's the door." He points to the entrance. "This is a TEAM sport and if you want to be a part of this team, stop being a douche."

The rest of the team all nods in agreement. Däuchmen, looks around and when he realizes that no one is sticking up for him, he stands up in a huff, pushing his chair back, knocking it over from the force of him jumping up so quickly. "Fuck you all," he snarls and when he walks past me, he slams into my shoulder, causing me to stumble. "You're going down, Canada Boy."

He exits the bar, slamming the door in his haste, once again garnering the attention of everyone in the bar, Chelsea included. Our eyes once again lock but as quick as our gaze connects, she looks back to her friend, ignoring me.

JJ catches my attention and mouths, 'Go for it.' Nodding at him, I turn and pretend I'm heading toward the bar but at the last minute, I spin and make a beeline for Chels.

It's as if someone is on my side because she's alone at her table. Continuing over to her, my heart begins to race. I've never been nervous around the opposite sex before, but I've never been interested in the coach's daughter before either.

Stopping by her table, I stare down at her. She looks absolutely radiant tonight but then again, she always does.

She stares back at me, blinking rapidly. Her mouth opens and closes but nothing comes out, she's mute.

"Howz it goin', Chels?" *Really, Jones, that's what you open with?*

"It's going good," she finally says after what feels like an eternity of silence. "What are you guys doing here? I thought you had practice?"

"Team bonding session."

She nods. "Ohh. And how's that going?"

"Well, Däuchmen stormed out and I'm over here talking to you."

"Ohh...and why are you over here talking to me?"

"I...I was hoping to take you out? Coffee? Dinner? Brunch? Your choice."

"I can't—"

"Nope," I interrupt and take the seat next to her. "You can and you know why you can?"

"Why?"

"Because I like you, Chelsea Maxwell, and I think you like me too but you're scared to open up to me because you think I'm like Doucheman but I guarantee you, I'm nothing like that jackass."

"So, I'm just to take your word that you're not like him."

"I can call my nanna and she can vouch for me."

"And who's to say your nanna wouldn't lie for you?"

"Would your nanna lie to someone on your behalf?" She shakes her head no. "And she's Canadian, it's like in our DNA not to lie, eh."

This causes her to laugh. "You have a beautiful laugh," I honestly tell her.

"Thank you. And, Kallen, I'd—"

"Oh My God," Margot screeches as she rejoins us. "You will never guess who..." She stops mid-sentence. "Ohh, I guess you already know." She sits across from Chelsea and me, leaning her elbows on the table, and resting her chin in her palms. "Sooo, what are we talking about?"

"I'm trying to get Chelsea here to go out with me," I inform her, hoping that her friend will help me here.

"Reeeeeally, and how's that going?"

"Well, I'm offering for her to speak to my nanna, who will vouch on my behalf that I'm a good guy."

"Couldn't your nanna just lie?" she repeats Chelsea's question from before.

"Apparently, nannas don't lie and she's Canadian," Chelsea deadpans.

"What's being Canadian got to do with it?"

"They can't lie, it's in their DNA."

"Well, they are nice people, and they always apologize, so he's kinda right there but nannas can still lie. Mine lies all the time."

"Nanna Radclyff has dementia, that's not lying."

"Semantics, but that aside, are you going to go out with the boy?"

"Yeah, Chels, are you going to go out with me?"

"Wow, nothing like putting a girl on the spot."

"Quit stalling," Margot snaps at her friend but before Chels can reply, she answers for her. "She's free Saturday night and she'll meet you at Jozo's in Hell's Kitchen at seven."

"Will I now?"

"Yes, yes you will." She looks to me. "That good with you?"

"Perfect." Looking to Chelsea, I smile. "I look forward to it." Leaning down, I press a kiss to her cheek. Standing up to full height, I look between them both. "Have a nice night, ladies."

And with that, I head back over to the team, excited for my date on Saturday night.

18

CHELSEA

"What the hell, Margot?" I chastise my soon-to-be ex-best friend after Kal leaves us. "What if I didn't want to go out with him?"

"You did," she nonchalantly replies, "you just needed a gentle nudge in the right direction." I eyeball my friend. "Look, you're never going to get over Doucheman if you don't skate back onto the rink. You already know he's great in the sack...and on the kitchen counter...so now's your chance to see if he's as great outside of the sexy schmexy, and for the record, I think he might be."

"Just 'cause he's Canadian, doesn't mean he's great."

"I'm not saying it's because he's Canadian. I'm saying it because he's still pursuing you, even knowing who your dad is, and a man THAT fine cannot have a mean bone in his body."

"Stop making sense of all of this. I thought you were my best friend?"

"I am and it's because of that that I'm pushing for this. Look, I haven't seen you this happy and excited about a guy in forever. I don't even think you were this gaga when you first started dating Doucheman." She pauses and then adds, "Focus on Kallen Jones the person. Not Kallen Jones the puckhead."

Focus on Kallen Jones the person. Not Kallen Jones the puckhead, that's some good advice there, who knew my bestie was so smart. "Fine," I relent. "I will go into this with an open mind but if it bites me in the ass, I'm totally blaming you...and tequila. Now, let's get our beer on and stop talking about puckheads."

"Deal, but before we close the Kallen and puckheads convo for tonight, I just need to point out that he hasn't stopped staring at you since he went back over to the team."

Turning my head, sure enough, I catch him staring at me. He's not fazed at being busted for staring, if anything, he seems proud to have been caught. He winks and that one little action, from all the way across the bar, causes my body to zing to life and my heart to flutter. I haven't felt like this, since well, our first night together and now, I'm excited for our date on Saturday, not that I'm confirming that to Margot. But first, we need to survive the team dinner on Friday with *him* and my dad.

The next few days fly by and before I know it, I'm walking into the team dinner on Friday night. I may have pre-gamed with a few wines while I was getting ready, and I might be slightly tipsy, but I need all the courage I can for tonight. Of course, fate decides to live up to her bitchy moniker because the first person I see when I enter the private dining room is *him*.

"Looking good, Chels. Ready to come back to me yet?" *he* arrogantly voices.

"Has hell frozen over yet?" I snap at him.

"Just give up and come back, you know you want to."

"I would rather shove a cactus up my ass than be with you. Now run along and leave me alone."

"Get away from my daughter, Däuchmen," Dad growls, swooping in to my rescue, not that I need it because I can handle *him*. I'm no damsel in distress. "And I do believe I heard her say to leave her alone."

"You can't protect her forever, old man," Stefan snarls at Dad, this man has guts, I'll give him that.

"Watch your mouth, boy," Dad growls at him. "As soon as I get the opportunity to trade your sorry ass, you're out. You're only still on this team because legally my hands are tied."

"Whatever, as soon as I get the chance to leave, I am. This team is a joke." He shakes his head. "I made my appearance, I'm out of here." He turns on his heel to exit but the door to the room opens and in walks Kallen. He looks amazing tonight in dress pants, a white button-down, and a tie. "Watch it, Canada Boy." He shoulder-barges Kallen, causing him to stumble before he storms out of the room.

Racing over, I rest my palm on Kal's forearm. "Kal, you okay?"

"Fine, he's such a..."

"Douche," I finish for him. "His last name certainly is on point for his personality."

Kal laughs at my comment. "You and the majority of the world think that." Now it's my turn to laugh. Once the laugher stops, we stare at one another. The air around us crackles, just like each and every time we are near one another.

"You look beautiful, Chels," he tells me, his eyes once again raking over me and unlike when *he* did it earlier, I don't shudder. Tonight I'm wearing a simple, deep purple wrap dress and black wedge sandals. My hair has been straightened and the golden locks hang down my back.

"You look pretty good yourself," I honestly tell him, straightening up his tie. He always looks good but tonight, in this, hot-hot-hot comes to mind.

"Jones, good of you to make it," Dad interrupts us, but I'm kind of thankful for it as I was a few seconds away from throwing myself at him.

"It's good to be here, sir."

"Call me Coach or David." I roll my eyes at the clichéness of that but at the same time, I'm not surprised by Dad's response.

"I'll stick with Coach."

"And who is this young man?" Mom asks, joining us. She kisses my cheek and then slides her arm around Dad's waist. The two of them are hopelessly in love with one another, I'm surprised that I don't have a billion siblings. They can never keep their hands off one another, and I've lost count of the number of times I've heard them getting it on or walked in on them getting it on. I think from age fifteen, I NEVER sat on the sofa 'cause I didn't need to be sitting where my parents just did that.

"Nessa, this is Kallen Jones. Our new goalie. Kallen, this here is my lovely wife, Vanessa."

"Pleasure to meet you, ma'am." He offers Mom his hand, but Mom being Mom, pulls him in for a hug. I can't help but laugh at the shocked expression on Kal's face right now.

"You're the Canadian?" Mom asks him.

Kal nods. "Yep, that's me, ma'am."

"Please, call me Nessa. Ma'am is so old-fashioned and I'm not old...yet."

"I can see where your daughter gets her good looks from," Kallen tells Mom. She smiles and my eyes widen at his not so subtle flirting.

"Ohh, stop." Mom slaps Kal on the chest, all embarrassed, but I know for a fact that she's loving this. Mom loves when people think that we're sisters and not mother/daughter.

"Kal's right, Nessa, you are just as pretty today as you were when we first met and our daughter, thankfully, got your looks and not mine."

"I still think you look pretty good," Mom replies to Dad with that look in her eye, and I give them twenty minutes before she drags him into a supply closet for them to get it on.

"Come on, Kal, let's get a drink." Reaching out, I grab his hand in mine and drag him away from Mom and Dad, but they are so engrossed in each other, they don't even notice that we've left them alone.

Stopping at the bar, I order a wine for myself and look to Kal. "What'll it be?"

"Tequila," he matter-of-factly states, and that one word has my vagina buzzing. My eyes widen and he steps closer to me, leans down, and whispers, "I keep thinking about that night." His breath hits my heated skin causing goose pimples. I stare at the lit-up bar, frozen. "Every time I'm in my kitchen, I get a hard-on thinking about all the sexy and delicious things I did to your body on my countertop."

Resting my palm on his chest, his muscular chest that I remember licking and sucking tequila off of, I lift my gaze to his. "I think about that night too," I huskily confirm.

"You do, do you?"

Nodding, I bite my lip and before my brain kicks into gear, I pant, "Maybe we need a replay?"

19
KALLEN

Maybe we need a replay, five fan-fucking-tabolous words to hear but before I can agree to a replay, the Coach taps on his beer bottle, garnering everyone's attention.

"Thank you all for coming this evening. The Crushers are not just a team, we're a family and I couldn't do this without my wife Nessa, or our daughter, Chelsea. Especially Chelsea. Come over here, Pumpkin." Reluctantly, she walks over to her dad. When she reaches him, he pulls her into his side and kisses the side of her head. "Right now, my baby girl has stepped up and really helped with my office," we all laugh at that because his office was a bomb before Chels swooped in, "and the general running of things." A round of applause erupts for Chelsea. With claps and whistles, myself cheering the loudest. "All right, all right," Coach shouts. "With that said, let's crush it this season—"

"That jokes still shit, Coach," Jett chortles and everyone nods in agreement.

"That bench is looking mighty good for you, Jensen."

"Carry on, sir," Jett quickly says. Raising his beer to Coach in defeat, he sits back in his chair and from the look on his face, he thinks Coach is serious.

"As I was saying, let's crush it this season and let's bring The Cup back to New York."

The room erupts once again, I really have scored a position on the best team. Not only on the ice but off it too, bar one person, but one person cannot bring this team down.

My eyes focus on Chelsea and as if there's an invisible force pulling us together, her gaze lands on mine. She smiles and I can't help myself, I grin back and then I mouth the word 'replay' to her. Her cheeks darken and she bites her lip, but the joke's once again on me because my cock begins to throb. *Fuck,* I internally groan. Subtly, I rearrange my junk and try to focus on Coach, but my eyes keep drifting to the angel standing beside him.

JJ slides in next to me and whispers, "There's drool on your chin." Lifting my hand, I wipe but there's nothing there. Looking to JJ, I see him grinning.

"Asshole," I whisper-growl and then elbow him in the stomach.

"Uggh, that's a wicked elbow you have there."

"Thanks," I nonchalantly tell him with a shrug. "Now, shhhh, Coach is talking."

"Suck hole," he teases, but he's right, I need to keep on his good side if I'm going to give this a shot with Chelsea.

Finally, Coach wraps up his speech, we all clap and cheer and then the waiters walk in with trays and trays of food, filling up the buffet. The smell alone makes my mouth water. I'm glad this isn't a sit-down dinner because it means I have a chance to chat with Chelsea.

Biding my time, I wait until she's at the buffet and then quickly race over. Grabbing a plate, I stand next to her. "Fancy meeting you here."

She turns her head to look at me. "Can you get any cheesier than that?"

"Well, I could but I think we both know that I don't need a pick-up line to woo you, you're already smitten."

"Cocky much?"

"You know my cock—" She covers my mouth with her hand.

"I don't need to be thinking about your cock right now."

"How about later?"

"Maybe," she says with a cheeky wink. Placing a chicken skewer on her plate, she turns and walks over to her mom and dad, adding an extra sway to her ass with each step she takes away from me.

"You are so screwed," JJ teases, slapping me on the shoulder, joining me at the buffet. He picks up a plate and begins filling it with enough food to feed a family of four.

"Hungry?"

"Famished," he replies, shoving a spring roll into his mouth. "This will be the last time I get to eat all the fried goodness for the rest of the season," he says with a mouthful, "so I'm stocking up and enjoying it before it's chicken and broccoli and protein shakes for the foreseeable future."

"You know you don't have to eat so boringly. I can hook you up with my nutritionist. He prepares meals for me for the week that are to die for yummy and fit in with the calorie and dietary requirements. All I have to do is nuke it in the oven and BOOM, amazing dinner for one."

"That'd be great, dude. I suck at cooking, hence the chicken and broccoli diet. You can't fuck that up."

"I'll get his deets to you when I get home."

"Thanks, man, appreciate it." Before he walks away, he adds another three spring rolls and four chicken skewers to his plate.

Shaking my head, I walk over to a vacant table and begin to eat. Nessa Maxwell joins me just as I finish eating. "How are you enjoying living in the States?" she asks, taking a sip of her white wine.

"It's great, but I do miss my sister and grandparents."

"What about your parents?"

"They probably don't even realize that I don't live in Canada anymore. Pops and Nanna pretty much raised Kendall and me."

"They sound like wonderful people...your grandparents, that is."

"They're the best and are looking forward to flying down for the first game of the season."

"They can join me in the team box," she offers.

Shaking my head, I smile. "Thank you for the offer but they have floor seats. They love to sit rinkside so they can be in the thick of it. Pops has never missed a game of mine."

"Just like I've never missed one of David's games, not even when I was pregnant with Chels. I came close to giving birth to her rinkside. My contractions began at the beginning of the last period of the final Cup game. I wasn't going to miss seeing David win his first Cup. As soon as that buzzer went off and they'd won, I called a cab and went to the hospital. I sent him a text telling him what was happening and on the last push, he barreled into the delivery room and managed to see the arrival of his daughter."

"Wow, what an arrival."

"Yep, we named her after his coach, Raymond Chelsea."

"That's so cool. I love when people's names have a meaningful story behind them."

"Any meaning behind yours?"

Shaking my head. "Nah, well, not that I know of anyway."

We both fall silent, then Nessa looks intently at me. "You're good for her."

My eyes widen at her words, and I choke on the sip of beer I just took. "Excuse me?"

"Chels, you're just what she needs."

My mouth opens and closes. I'm at a loss for words right now. "How? What? How?"

Nessa laughs and it puts me at ease. "You two haven't been able to keep your eyes off one another all night and I'm her mom, I know my daughter. Just don't mess with her heart."

Shaking my head sideways, I look intently at Nessa. "No way in hell will I hurt her." Looking over my shoulder, my eyes find Chels and she's watching us. Winking at her, I turn back to Nessa. "She's perfect in every way, Nessa."

"Good," she states matter-of-factly, "David might be your coach and scary, but I guarantee you, I'm scarier. A mother will do anything to protect her child and Chelsea is my everything. Just remember that."

"Duly noted...any tips on winning her over?"

"Just be you. You seem like a lovely young man, and she's already smitten. Don't give up on her, I'm sure you know what happened with—"

"Yeah, I do and he's a dick, pardon my language, ma'am, for doing that to her. I would never cheat on her. When, not if, she lets me in, I'll protect her to the best of my ability."

"She just needs to be loved," Nessa says, smiling at me.

The air around us changes and I sense her before I see her. Chels joins me. "So, what are you two talking about?"

"Your arrival into this world," Nessa tells her, her face beaming. She really does love her daughter.

"Ohh, Mom, no. Really?"

"Don't worry," she adds, "I didn't tell him that you still sleep with your teddy."

"Mooooom, stop." She looks to me. "She's joking about the teddy."

"No, I'm not," her mom teases. "I'll leave you both to it, it was lovely chatting with you, Kallen, and remember what I said."

"It's locked away, Nessa." I tap my temple. "It was lovely chatting with you too."

She squeezes Chelsea's arm and walks away, leaving me alone with her daughter. "So, what did you two discuss?"

"If I told you, I'd have to kill you, and I'd rather not do that because for starters, I look horrendous in orange. But most of all, I don't want to kill you because I want to get to know you better and get you to fall hopelessly in love with me."

"I think you'd rock the orange, as for falling in love, not planning on doing that again anytime soon."

"We'll see," I state. "So, you ready for our replay?"

She bites her bottom lip as she steps closer to me and whispers, "Only if we can stop and get tequila."

"I think that can be arranged, Ms. Maxwell."

"Let me say goodbye to Mom and Dad and then we can go."

"Well, we can't leave together, that will arouse suspicion." She nods in agreement. "Let me say goodbye first and then you can follow me."

"Sounds like a plan." She walks away from me and joins her parents. I shake my head, not quite believing that I'm going to get a second chance with her.

Walking over to her and her parents, I stretch out my hand to Coach. "Thank you for a great evening, Coach, and, Nessa, but I'm going to head home now."

"Chels was just saying she was ready to go too. Why don't you guys split a cab?" Nessa suggests, pushing us together, unofficially playing matchmaker.

"You mind escorting my daughter home, Jones?"

"Not at all, sir. As long as she doesn't mind?"

"I'm a grown woman, I can make my way home."

"Humor me, Pumpkin," her dad says, pulling her into his side and kissing her on the head.

"Fine," she relents. She looks to me. "Kallen, I would love for you to escort me home."

We both say our goodbyes and the two of us exit the restaurant. If you told me earlier tonight as I was getting ready that I'd be leaving this dinner with Chelsea Maxwell, I would have told you to put down the crack pipe. But here we are, and I guarantee you, I'm going to make sure she has the best night ever and then tomorrow night at Jozo's, it can be our first official date.

I'm not letting this second chance go, no pucking way.

20

CHELSEA

As I walk out with Kallen by my side, I think about Mom pushing us together. Looking over at him when we stop on the street and wait to hail a taxi I ask, "What exactly did you and my mom talk about?"

"Your arrival. My nonparents. My sister and grand-parents. The usual get to know you stuff. Why?"

"She seems to be pushing us together."

"Maybe she just knows that you and I are meant to be, Chels. Mom's intuition and all that jazz."

"Why do I feel there's something that you aren't telling me?"

"I have no clue." A taxi pulls up and he opens the door for me to climb in. A crack resonates in the night air, he just slapped my ass as I climbed in. I squeal and giggle, and just like our first night together, the stinging of my ass has me soaking my panties with arousal.

Sitting next to him, he looks over at me and I feel like

I'm transported back in time. "I'm having a déjà vu moment right now."

"I may have slapped your ass that first night too," he confirms my thoughts.

"So what else are you going to do like the first night, Kallen Jones?"

He leans over. His heated breath hits my neck, causing my skin to break out in goosebumps. "Everything, Chelsea Maxwell, I'm going to do everything to you when we get back to my place." And if memory serves me correctly, he said that too. This feels like a do-over, but this time will it end with me sneaking out like a skanky ho? Only time will tell.

Swallowing deeply, I clench my thighs together at his words. His voice is deep and vibrates through my body. It comes alive, thrumming with desire and want for this man. I've never been more turned on than I am right now.

The taxi comes to a stop and when I look out the window, I realize we're at his place. I was so lost in my desire and internal thoughts the trip flew by. We enter the building and stop by the front desk, and Phil, the same clerk from the first night I came back with him, hands Kallen a brown paper bag. "Here you go, sir."

"Thanks, Phil," Kallen says, taking the bag from him. "Have a good night."

He takes my hand in his and we walk toward the elevators. "What's in the bag?" I ask as we wait for it to arrive.

Kallen looks over to me. "Tequila." Once again, my body comes alive.

"Tequila," I repeat. "My favorite drink, I hope I can drink it from my favorite cup."

"And what cup would that be?"

"You." Just as I say that the doors open and I step in. Turning around, I notice he's still standing there. "You coming?"

He nods and smirks. "Nothing would stop me, and I think I can find that cup for you." He steps in and stalks toward me, causing me to step backward. My back hits the cool glass of the metal car's mirror. My breath hitches as he cocoons my body with his. The doors close and the air thickens around us the closer he presses himself into me. I can feel his cock pushing into me, and once again, I have to squeeze my thighs together and hold back the moan wanting to escape.

How this man can turn me to mush just by staring at me boggles my mind, but when he cups my cheek in his palm and stares into my soul, I'm lost to him. Then he ups the ante by whispering, "You are so beautiful, Chels."

Before I can reply, the elevator dings, signaling our arrival. He takes my hand in his and we step out into the hallway and turn toward his door. The door at the other end opens. "Yo, fuckface, how was—" The voice stops mid-sentence, both Kallen and I turn toward it. "Ohh, hello," he says, walking toward us. "I'm Pearce."

"And we're busy," Kallen dismisses his neighbor.

"Don't be rude," I scold him. Pulling my hand free, I turn to face who I now know as Pearce. "Hi, Pearce, I'm Chelsea." I stretch out my hand.

"Chelsea, it's a pleasure." He pulls my hand to his lips and presses a gentle kiss to my knuckles. His lips linger longer than necessary, and I notice his eyes are on Kallen, clearly, he's doing this to piss Kal off.

"Back off, Pearce," Kal growls from behind me.

"Down, boy," I tease him. Pulling my hand free from Pearce, I turn and press my hand to Kal's chest. "Kal, Pearce here is just being nice."

"Yeah, Kal, I'm just being nice," he teases back, clearly these two are friends.

"Aaaaand that's going too far," I inform him.

"Ha," Kal retorts. I look up at him with raised eyebrows. "What?" he replies, feigning ignorance.

Shaking my head, I turn back to Pearce. "Do you want to join us?"

Pearce's eyes widen and then I realize how sexual that sounded so I quickly tack on, "For a drink. Do you want to join Kal and me for a drink?"

"Thanks for the drink"—he places emphasis on the word drink—"invitation, but I'm heading out to meet the guys. When I heard the elevator, I thought I'd invite Kal but I see he has better company, so I'll leave you two to your drink." Once again, he places emphasis on the word drink.

"It was lovely to meet you," I tell him as Kal yells, "Catch ya around, man." He takes my hand in his and pulls, well drags, me toward his door.

"Don't be rude," I whisper-shout.

"I'm not, I just want to get you alone."

"So we can have drinks?" I tease.

He bursts out laughing, "Come on." He pushes the door open, and I step past him into his apartment and just like the first night I was here, I'm mesmerized by the view before me.

"You really have a great apartment."

"Thanks, as soon as I saw it, I had to have it."

"The view alone would have sold it for me, but it also has a dream kitchen and don't get me started on your master bath."

"Sooo, you only like me for my apartment?"

"And the glass you offer when drinking tequila."

"Speaking of, would you like a drink?"

"Just water to start, please."

"One water coming up." He walks into the kitchen, placing the brown paper bag on the countertop. He grabs a bottle from the refrigerator, and I take a seat on the stool under the counter, spinning side to side nervously. Sliding the bottle across to me, I uncap it and take a sip.

Kal walks around the counter, coming to a stop next to me. Turning my head to face him, he lifts his hand and brushes a tendril of hair behind my ear. Cupping my cheeks, he leans forward and gently presses his lips to mine. My eyes close and I give myself over to the kiss. My lips open and he takes the opportunity to slip his tongue into my mouth. Our tongues slip and slide together.

Spinning my chair to face him, he slides his hands down to my ass and in one swift motion, lifts me into his arms. Instinctively, my legs wrap around his waist. He walks through the living room and out onto the outdoor terrace. Lowering himself down onto the end of the chaise lounge, I straddle him and continue to kiss him. Unabashedly, I grind myself on his growing erection. "Please," I whisper against his lips.

"Please, what?"

"Please make me come." I feel like such a hussy asking that but this man, he does things to me that I can't explain and right now, I need to come.

Slipping his hand between us, he slides it up my thigh and covers my mound with his palm, pressing down. The warmth of his skin through my panties feels amazing. "Your panties are soaked."

"Yep...please," I beg again. I sound like a whiny bitch right now, but I need to come like I need my next breath. He senses my need because he pushes my panties aside and presses a finger inside me. "Yes," I mewl, my head dropping back as he begins to thrust his finger in and out of me. He licks up the column of my neck and adds a second finger. Rocking myself on his hand, I grip his cheeks in my palms and press my lips to his. Our tongues battle it out in sync with his fingers plunging in and out of me.

Out of nowhere, I explode and climax all over his fingers. Throwing my head back, I moan and howl into the night sky as pleasure erupts throughout my body. The last of my body tremors subside and he removes his fingers from me.

"Thank you," I breathlessly pant.

"Happy to help you anytime."

Nodding, I shimmy back off his legs and drop to my knees. With my eyes locked on his, I lift my hands and begin to undo his belt. Licking my lips, I murmur, "My turn."

21
KALLEN

Before I can process what's happening, Chelsea has my cock free and her hand wrapped around the base. The tip glistens with my arousal. Her tongue darts out and she licks the liquid from the tip before opening wide, sucking me deep into her mouth. My shaft slides between her lips, the head hitting the back of her throat before she slides it back out again. She repeats the process over and over and over again.

My balls tingle and as much as it pains me, I push her off my cock. "If you keep that up, I'm gonna come."

"Isn't that the end goal of a blow job?"

"It is, but..."

"But what?" she asks, squeezing my thighs, reassuring me that whatever I say will be okay.

"I don't just want this," I flick my finger between us, "to just be about sex. I want it all with you."

"And you'll get that, right after you let me finish you off and you come down my throat."

Shaking my head, I cup her cheek. "You really are something, Chelsea Maxwell."

"As are you, now sit back and let me finish what I started."

Who am I to deny a sexy woman wanting to blow me? So, I do exactly as I'm told. I lean back on my arms and let her finish what she started. I was already close to coming so it doesn't take long before I'm fisting her hair in my hand and coming down her throat. She swallows every last drop. My cock springs free from her mouth, and she wipes the side of her lips with her finger, sucking the tip into her mouth.

"You keep that up and I'll fuck you right here, right now."

"Promises, promises," she teases.

Reaching out, I grab under her arms and lift her onto my lap. She straddles me again and we stare intently at one another. "How did I get so lucky to get a second chance with you?"

She shrugs and then whispers, "Just don't hurt me." If I wasn't staring at her, I would have missed it, she whispered it so quietly.

"Never." Sliding my hand around the back of her head, I pull her forward for a sweet and sensual kiss. Our tongues caress each other's, she pushes on my shoulder and I fall to the chaise cushion. Without breaking our connection, I shimmy us up to the pillows and flip her onto her back. She squeals and I stare down at her. "You are perfect."

"So you keep saying." She reaches up and cups my cheek. "Tell me everything I need to know about Kallen Jones."

Climbing off her, I roll to my back, tuck my junk back into my pants and I begin to tell her all about me, Kendall, and life in Vancouver. She cuddles into my side and listens to every word I tell her.

"So they just stopped parenting?"

"Pretty much," I confirm with a nod. "Nanna and Pops stepped in and the rest is history."

"I'm so glad you had Nanna, Pops, and Kendall."

"Me too and to be honest, I'm not upset that our parents did what they did because Kendall and I still had a great childhood, thanks to the awesomeness that is Nanna and Pops."

"I'd love to meet them."

"And you will. They're flying down for the first game of the season with Kendall. Kendall is a diehard Crushers fan. She has been since forever."

"I'll be sure to hook her up with some team merchandise."

"She'd love that, and you will forever be her best friend if you do that."

"Consider it done." A yawn follows her statement.

"I think I need to get you to bed."

She rolls half on top of me. "Is that your way of asking me to sleep with you?"

"I guess it is, but I meant to sleep-sleep, not sleep with you sleep, but for the record, I'm totally open to the sleep with you sleep option too."

She leans forward and presses her lips to mine,

pulling back, she rests her forehead against mine. "I guess we could sleep together sleep before we sleep-sleep together."

"You had me at sleep."

In one swift motion, I pick her up in my arms bridal-style and walk us inside and up to my bedroom. Placing her on her feet at the end of the bed, I grab the hem of her dress and, ever so slowly, lift it over her head. Dropping it to the floor, I step back and appreciate her in her underwear. "You are exquisite."

She ducks her head in embarrassment. Placing my finger under her chin, I lift her gaze to mine. "Don't go all shy on me when I compliment you."

"I'm just not used to it."

"Well, get used to it, baby, because I will tell you every day how perfect and beautiful you are."

"You, Kallen Jones, are the sweetest man I have ever met."

"Shhhh, don't tell anyone. You'll ruin my puckhead reputation."

"Your secret is safe with me, now are we going to sleep or what?"

"Or what, what?"

"Not this again." She rests her hand on her hip and cocks it to the side. "Am I going to have to do this myself?"

"That could also work. I think it would be hot to watch you pleasure yourself. You up for the challenge?"

She nods. "But there's one problem in this scenario."

"And what's that?"

"You," she points her finger at me, "have too many clothes on."

"So do you." She looks down at herself.

"Ummm, I'm in a bra and panties. You are in pants, a shirt, and briefs."

"That's easily fixed." Reaching behind my neck, I grab the collar of my shirt and pull it over my head.

"That's hot," Chelsea breathlessly whispers.

"What's hot?" I ask as I remove my pants, leaving me in my briefs.

"When a guy removes his shirt like that."

"Duly noted to remove shirt like that from now on, but we seem to have another problem now."

"And what might that problem be?" She reaches behind her back and unclasps her bra, her tits falling free and her nipples pebbling when the cool air hits them.

"I was going to say, you are now overdressed but you just evened up the playing field. We are now both down to one item."

"That we are. On three we remove them?"

"Deal."

"One," she utters.

"Two," I count.

"Three," we both voice.

Each of us hook our fingers into the material of the said clothing and pull them off, leaving both of us naked as the day we were born. My eyes roam over her body and the saucy minx runs her fingertip between the valley of her breasts, circling the tip over her stomach. Getting lower and lower with each circle, she turns around and sits on the end of my bed. Shuffling up toward the pillows, she settles back and opens her thighs, giving me an unobstructed view of her pussy. Her lips are glistening with her arousal, her finger slides through her slit easily. Her head drops back and she moans as she slips her finger inside her.

"Eyes on me," I growl.

Lifting her head, her eyes focus on my face until she notices what I'm doing to myself. Her gaze rakes down my body and homes in on my dick. Gripping my shaft tighter, I begin to languidly stroke myself up and down.

"Don't stop," I inform her. "We do this together."

She nods and bites her lip as she begins to finger herself and squeeze her tit with her other hand.

We both continue to pleasure ourselves in front of one another. I know she's close when her breathing becomes hurried. "I'm close," she whispers, confirming that I read her body correctly.

"Let go," I demand and let go she does. She pinches her nipple, rolling the tip between her thumb and forefinger as she pumps her fingers in and out. "Yessssssss," she mewls as she crashes over the edge.

Seeing her let loose like that lights the fire within me and I too come. Milky strands spray all over my hand and the end of my bed.

"Now, that was smokin' hot," she informs me, removing her hand from between her thighs. Lifting her fingers to her mouth, she wraps her lips around her digits and licks her arousal off them.

"No, *that* is hot." Bending down, I pick up my shirt and wipe off my hand and the end of the bed.

Dropping it back to the floor, I climb onto the bed

and stalk up her body. "I think that is my new favorite way of pleasuring myself. Watching you bring yourself to climax is the sexiest thing I've ever seen."

"Watching you was pretty erotic too, but right now, I need to sleep-sleep."

"I'm scared to go to sleep," I honestly tell her as I lie down next to her.

"Why?"

"The last time I went to sleep in a bed with you, I woke up and you were gone."

She rolls to her side and cups my cheek. "I promise that I'll still be here in the morning."

"I'll hold you to that." Turning my head, I place a kiss on her palm and cover her hand with mine. We lie on our sides, hands cupped on my cheek, and we fall asleep together. Sated and blissfully happy.

22

KALLEN

Waking the next morning, I lie here for a few moments before I open my eyes, memories of the last time and waking up alone flash before my closed eyelids. Cracking open one eye, I smile when I see she's still here.

She's.

Still.

Here.

Chels and I are in the same position on our sides, still facing each other. She looks so peaceful right now. My gaze wanders over her face, my morning wood twitches when she moves and the sheet slips down, baring a taut pink nipple, giving me an unobstructed view of one breast.

I'm resisting the urge to lean over and suckle on it. Chels has the most amazing tits, and I hope that one day she'll let me fuck them. For someone who is a tit man, she is the first person I have been with to have an out of this world, incredible rack.

"Morning," she rasps and once again, my cock twitches.

Looking back up to her face, I see her smiling over at me. "Morning, gorgeous, sleep well?"

"Like the dead." She lifts her arms above her head and stretches, now both her tits are on display and my cock is rock fucking hard.

Leaning over, I go in for a morning kiss, but she covers her mouth. "I have morning breath," she informs me from behind her hand.

"Babe, I had your pussy in my mouth last night, I think I can handle morning breath."

"Well, when you put it like that, I'll happily take that morning kiss then."

Cupping her cheek with my palm, I lean over and press my lips to hers. I was only intending for it to be a quick good morning peck, but it turns into a full-on make-out session when she throws her arms over my shoulders, pulls me closer, and slips her tongue into my mouth.

Shuffling so I'm cocooning her underneath me, I slide my hand from her cheek down to her breast and cup it in my hand, gently massaging the plump mound, garnering a sweet moan from her.

Pulling back, I stare down at her and continue to fondle her tit. "You have the most perfect tits. One of these days, I'm going to fuck them."

She shocks me with the next three words she utters, "Why not now?"

"Because it's..."

"It's what?"

"I don't know."

"Then have at it." She pushes my hand aside and presses her tits together. I groan at the sight before me and I quickly pull the sheet off the bed and straddle her abdomen. She beckons me forward with her finger. "Let me suck it first and get it all wet."

"Fuuuuck, you're going to be the death of me."

"But what a way to go," she cheekily replies. "Now come here and let me suck your dick."

Not wanting to anger her, or miss out on my ultimate fantasy, I do as she asks. Reaching down, I begin to stroke my dick before I shimmy myself up her body, circling her nipple with the weeping head of my dick as I slide past. Chels opens her mouth and sucks my shaft into her mouth. "Fuuuuck me," I growl as she increases the pressure on my dick. "If you keep that up, babe, I'm gonna come in your mouth and right now, I want my ultimate fantasy to come true and fuck your tits."

"Mmmhmpf," she mumbles, her tongue scraping up the underside of my shaft with the vibration of her agreement.

Reluctantly, I pull myself out of her mouth and shuffle back down her body as she pushes her tits back together, awaiting my cock. She raises her eyebrows at me and breathlessly whispers, "Have at it, baby."

Dropping my gaze to her chest, I push my hips forward and press the tip between her breasts. She begins to massage her tits, trapping my cock between them as I thrust my hips back and forth. The sensation is amazing and the amazingness increases when she lifts herself up and licks the head of my shaft when he pokes out the other side. "Fuuuuck," I grunt as I begin to pick up speed.

My balls tighten and I know I'm close. This is the most amazing thing ever and when my eyes land on Chels, she looks to be enjoying this just as much as I am.

"I'm gonna come," I warn her and on the next slide through, I explode. White hot strings of cum burst free, coating her chin, as her breasts continue to milk every last drop from me.

Both of us are heavily breathing when she lets go of her breasts and my dick rests between them. We stare at one another while we catch our breath.

"Was that everything you wanted it to be?" she asks me, wiping a bit of cum off her chin before sucking her finger into her mouth.

"Everything and more. You, Chelsea Maxwell, are full of surprises."

"Good surprises, I hope?"

"Very good surprises." Dropping back to the mattress beside her, I roll to my side and rest my head in my palm. My gaze roams over her chest and seeing her marked with my seed does something to me. "Guess I should get you in the shower."

"Ready for round two already?"

"With you, always."

"Your stamina is amazing; I can see why Dad hired you."

"Let's not talk about your dad when my cum is all over your naked tits, actually, let's never talk about your dad when we're naked."

"Deal, now let's get clean so we can get dirty again."

"What have I unleashed?"

"The new and improved Chelsea." She smiles at me and sits on the edge of the bed. She glances over her shoulder and stares down at me. "Thank you for bringing me back to life, Kallen, and...and for not giving up on me."

"No need to thank me, plus it should be me thanking you for taking a chance on another puckhead, but I promise you, I will never hurt you. Intentionally or otherwise. I look after what's mine and you, Chelsea Maxwell, are mine."

"And you, Kallen Jones, are mine but please, don't puck me over. I won't handle being pucked over again."

"Not in a million years will I puck you over. I will puck you and kiss you and maybe one day even love you, but for now, I'll treat you like the amazing woman you are." And that's the truth, I've never felt this way about someone before and Chelsea is definitely someone I can see myself falling in love with.

23

CHELSEA

Kallen and I are lying on the sofa binging the *Fast and Furious* movies, I know when we get to number seven, I'm gonna bawl like a baby at the end because I'm still not over Paul Walker's death. Why do the good always die young?

After our amazing wake-up sex—FYI, his cock sliding through my boobs was the most amazing and erotic feeling ever. We jumped in the shower and before we got clean, we got dirty again. That little shower bench is ah-may-zing, Kal sat on it, and I straddled him backward, and then I leaned on it and he took me from behind. This man is a god with the stick between his legs. I don't think my va-jay-jay has ever seen so much action in such a short period of time.

Lying here with my back to his front is the perfect way to spend a Saturday afternoon.

"So, tonight," he says, placing a kiss just below my

ear. "I'm supposed to be taking you to Jozo's so we can hopefully reunite, but since you took advantage of me last night—"

Looking over my shoulder, I stare at him feigning innocence. "Who took advantage of who?"

"Ummm. If I remember correctly, you were all grindy grindy on my lap when I carried you outside, begging me to make you come."

"Semantics."

"What if we go with, we both took advantage of each other because I can unequivocally say, you can take advantage of me anytime you like."

"Ditto," I confirm, a smile breaking out on my face. This is what I love about Kallen, everything is so easy and carefree.

He winks and then, being the innocent person he's claiming to be, he slides his hand down my body. He slips his fingers under the hem of my, well his shirt, grabbing his wrist, I halt his movements. "As much as I just said anytime, think we can give it a rest? My va-jay-jay is a little tender right now and I'd like to be able to walk tomorrow."

"Shit, I'm so sorry, why didn't you tell me to stop?"

"Because I liked what we were doing."

"But—"

Rolling over to face him, I squeeze his chin between my thumb and index finger. "You listen to me, and you listen good, Kallen Jones, I'm fine. Just a little tender. If you hurt me, I'll let you know."

"But—"

Shaking my head, I pinch his chin this time. "No, no buts."

He slides his hand around and squeezes my ass. "Ever?"

"Trust you to go there but yes, well no, no butt stuff. Ever. It's a one-way passage and that way is out and not in."

"But everything else is fair game?"

"Yep," I reply, letting the 'p' pop.

"Okay, got it. No butt stuff." He pauses. "Since you're out of action down there," he points down to my nether region, "can we make out?"

"I think I can handle that."

He places his hands on either side of my head and guides my lips to his. The kiss starts out soft and slow but then quickly turns heated and carnal. Before I know what's happening, I push him to his back, free his cock from his pants, tear my shirt over my head and ride him on the sofa, so much for a broken va-jay-jay.

We both come, screaming each other's name, and then I collapse on top of him. Both of us breathing heavily.

"I thought you were sore?" he voices, breaking the silence except for a *Fast and Furious* movie playing in the background.

"I was," I mumble into his chest, "and now I'm super sore but totally worth it." Lifting my head up, I rest my arms on his pecs and stare down at him. "You really know how to wield that stick in your pants."

"I'm good with my stick on and off the ice."

"Must you turn that into a hockey reference?"

"I'm a hockey guy, it's what we do."

"Gah, why did I fall for a puckhead?"

"Because you have great taste in men."

Not always, I immediately think but then quickly shake that thought away because I will not let *him* ruin this. I'm finally happy and this, what I have with Kallen, feels right. For some reason, I know that Kal won't do to me what *he* did. I need to forget all about *him* and focus on Kallen and us...and Paul Walker.

Rolling off Kal, we resume our position on the sofa—my back to his front, with him cupping my boobs, after making sure the girls were okay to touch—and spend the rest of the afternoon watching the *Fast and Furious* movies. Like I predicted, after number seven, I cry like a baby. Kal being the sweet man that he is, he held me while I cried and then carried me back to bed where I blissfully drifted off to la-la land wrapped in his embrace.

The sound of my phone ringing startles me and I accidentally headbutt Kallen when I wake up disoriented.

"Fuuuuck," he groans cupping his nose, blood seeping through his fingers.

Rolling over, I cup his face in my palms, "I'm so sorry, are you okay?"

"Nothing a bag of peas and some Tylenol won't fix," he mumbles through his hands.

Jumping out of bed, I race into his kitchen and grab a pack of peas from the freezer and a dishtowel. Wrapping the towel around them, I walk back in and sit on the edge of his bed and gently place it over his nose.

"Better?" I ask a few moments later. Pulling it back to

see that, thankfully, the blood flowing out of his nose seems to have stopped.

"Much. Feel free to play naked nurse like that anytime." He circles his finger at my nakedness and flicks my nipple and caresses my boob in his palm.

"Clearly you're fine if you're groping me."

"That wasn't a grope," he informs me. "This is a grope." He covers my breast and massages it. Closing my eyes, I drop my head back, enjoying the feeling of his hand on my breast. A moan slips free, but the moment is interrupted when my phone rings again.

"I better get that," I breathlessly whisper.

"Or let it go to voicemail and you can continue to play nurse, I've heard that sex is good for head injuries."

"Pretty sure they say to abstain from sex if you have a head injury."

"They don't know shit."

"Pretty sure the doctors and experts know what they're talking about."

"Whatevs, how—" But before he can try and convince me that sex is the best medicine for his head injury, my phone rings again.

"I really should get that."

Standing up, I walk out into the living room and pick up my phone. My eyes widen when I see five missed calls from Dad and two from Mom. Scrunching my face up, I shake my head and when I look up, my eyes widen when I see the time and I realize that I'm running late for brunch with my parents. I've been in a 'Kal bubble' for the last thirty-six hours nothing but him and his cock have been on my mind. Every Sunday we meet at a diner on Broadway for a family catchup and would you believe it, this diner is owned by a Canadian couple.

My phone rings again and thankfully it's Mom. "Mom, I'm so sorry," I say in greeting. "I've just woken up and I'm..." But I drift off, I can't tell her where I am in case Dad's in earshot.

"Dad's in the restroom," Mom informs me as if she can sense my inner turmoil. "I'll tell him you're on your way...and I think you should bring that lovely young man with you."

"How—" Of course Mom knows, she was playing matchmaker Friday night. "How did you know, Mom?"

"For starters, you two couldn't keep your eyes off each other on Friday night. Why do you think I pushed you two to leave together like I did?"

"I'm...I'm not ready for the official meet the parents yet, Mom, I just, we..."

"I'll leave it up to you to decide but I think you should be out in the open with this. Secrets never end well, so don't hide it. At the end of the day, your father wants you to be happy, even if that's with another one of his players."

"I-well-I, thank you."

"You can thank me in person when you both join us for brunch."

"What if Daddy kills him?"

"Leave your father to me. Just get here."

"Yes, Mom." Hanging up, I tap my phone on my chin, wondering how I broach this with Kallen. I'm so pucking scared right now.

24
KALLEN

L<small>YING IN BED WHILE</small> C<small>HELSEA ANSWERS HER PHONE</small>, I take a few moments to process all that's transpired in the last thirty-six hours. If you'd have told me Friday night that come Sunday morning Chelsea would still be here, I would have called you a big fat liar. As it was, I was still coming to terms with the shock of her agreeing to meet me at Jozo's last night but that went out of the window after Friday night.

A smile appears on my face when I hear her footsteps coming this way but when she steps into the room and I see her face ashen with worry, it quickly disappears. "What's wrong, babe? Is everything okay?"

"Yeah, it's all good. That was my mom, I'm late for Sunday brunch."

"Ohh," I utter. What more can I say? "I can drop you off if you like?"

"Ummm." She's hesitant right now and the happiness I felt earlier is quickly ebbing away.

"Umm, what?"

"Mom suggested that you join us."

"What?" I shout, shocked that her mom would want me there.

"Seems you made an impression on my mom on Friday night. She doesn't think we should hide this, us." She flicks her finger back and forth between us.

"And what do you think?"

"Well, I...I don't know. I'm not a fan of sneaking around 'cause that makes what we have seem wrong, and what we have doesn't feel wrong in any way, shape, or form. I know I tried to refuse us to begin with, but I know you're not *him* and I can't keep letting *him* dictate my life. And I don't want to hide my happiness."

"What about your dad?"

"Mom said she'll deal with him."

I nod my head processing her words and she's right, we don't need to hide this. We are adults. "I'd love to join you but, Chels." I hop off the bed and walk over to her. Placing one hand on her hip and with the other I pull her bottom lip free from her teeth, which are currently embedded deep into her flesh. "This is ultimately up to you. I will honor any decision you make, but if your dad so happens to kill me, please let my sister and grandparents know that my death wasn't in vain because I got to spend my last few hours with the most amazing woman in the world."

"Well, when you say romantic stuff like that, how can I not invite you along?"

"You can't, now let's get dressed because since you've mentioned food, I'm famished."

"Okay, let's do this, but can we swing by my place? I don't think I should turn up to a meet the parents' brunch wearing the same dress as I was wearing Friday night."

"I personally think that dress is hot, but I agree. I need to make a good impression and that sexy as sin dress won't help me achieve that." Then to lighten the heaviness of what's about to happen, I add, "You know, Coach already loves me as a player but also I need him to love me as the guy banging his daughter."

"You have such a way with words."

"I'm the complete package, now come and join me in the shower. So we can be all Earth conscious and save water."

"I didn't realize you were such an eco-warrior."

"I'm full of surprises, Chelsea Maxwell."

"That you are, Kallen Jones, that you are."

Thirty minutes later, after stopping by her place for Chels to change into jeans, a casual flowy tank, and a leather jacket, we park in a garage near the diner and head toward brunch where I'm about to officially meet Ness and Coach as more than just a player on his team. I'm meeting them as their daughter's boyfriend.

Chelsea and I walk hand in hand into the diner. As soon as she sees her parents, she drops my hand, and her breathing becomes ragged. Placing my hand on her lower back, we start walking toward them. Leaning in, I whisper, "Just breathe."

"I am," she replies through clenched teeth.

"Well, slow it down, otherwise you'll hyperventilate."

"I'm nervous all of a sudden."

"Nothing to be nervous about," I tell her, but when I look to the table, the stare and scowl on Coach's face tells me that maybe I should be nervous.

"Coach, Nessa," I offer in greeting when we reach the table.

"Hi, Daddy. Mom," Chelsea hurriedly says, kissing each of them on the cheek before heading into the booth across from them. My eyes drop to her denim-clad ass but the growl that comes from Coach quickly has me averting my gaze and sliding in next to Chelsea. I pick up the menu and focus on that and not on the confused-looking man across from me.

"So glad you could both join us," Nessa says, breaking the uncomfortable silence that's developed since we sat down.

"Thank you for inviting me," I reply with a smile.

"I didn't invite you," Coach growls. "I didn't even know you and my daughter are, well, whatever you are."

"Daaaaad," Chelsea cries. "Be nice."

"I am being nice. I just don't..." He shakes his head. His knuckles gripping the menu are bright white from squeezing the shit out of the laminated piece of paper. "Never mind what I thought. You wanna tell me what's going on? Was shocked when Ness said you'd be joining us."

"It's all kinda new, sir."

"Explain," he demands.

Looking over to Chels, I see a worried look on her face but for some inexplicable reason, now that I'm under the interrogation spotlight, I'm not nervous or scared facing off against the coach right now. Throwing her a wink, I look back to Coach. "I met your daughter before I officially started with the Crushers"—*and when I say met, I mean fucked the life out of her for twelve wonderful hours until she snuck off while I was sleeping, but he doesn't need to hear about that*—"and then we reconnected when I, well I guess we both started. At first, she refused to give me a chance because I'm a puckhead and we all know what the last puckhead did to her, but when I see something I want, I go after it. And I want to get to know more about this amazing woman sitting beside me, and thankfully, she lowered her guard and finally gave me a chance." Pausing, I look over to my girl and smile. Looking back to Coach, I stare him straight in the eye. "Chelsea is worth all the Russian bag skates that I'm sure you'll put me through if I hurt her but I promise, I won't, she's perfect in every way." FYI, bag skates are the worst and a Russian one is pure hell—skating from the goal line to blue line, back to goal line to center line, and so on.

No matter what Coach throws at me, I'll take it because I can see a future with Chels and I'll be damned if I'm going to screw it up.

Before anyone has a chance to comment on what I just said, our waitress arrives with her order pad in hand. "What can I get ya'll today?"

Coach goes first, "I'll have the French toast with a side of bacon."

Nessa orders next. "I'll have the same but no bacon on the side."

Then it's Chelsea's turn. "Eggs Benedict for me, please."

And then I'm up. "Breakfast poutine for me, thanks."

"Coming right up." She smiles and heads back to place our order.

"What the puck is breakfast poutine?" Chelsea questions me as soon as the waitress is out of earshot. Her face is scrunched in confusion and disgust at my brunch choice.

"Like the best breakfast meal out there. Maple smoked bacon, cheese curds, caramelized brandy onions, homemade fries swimming in gravy and hollandaise sauce, and topped off with poached eggs on top. I was surprised it was on the menu."

"That sounds disgusting," she fake gags. "And it would be because the owners are Canadian."

"Sounds like a heart attack waiting to happen," Coach says. "Better enjoy it now because once the season begins, there will be no more breakfast poutine for you, boy. It will be egg white omelets and spinach."

"And that's just as good. The chef who prepares my meals knows how to turn bland into grand."

"So apart from your horrible taste in breakfast foods, what else do I need to know about you before I allow you to date my daughter?"

"Daaaaad," Chelsea protests just as I throwback at Coach, "What do you want to know?" I'm not at all nervous to be thrown in the spotlight like this. I want this to go well, not just for me, but also for Chels. This is a huge step for her, and I'd hate to be the reason the relationship with her dad sours.

"Where did you grow up?"

"Vancouver." But he knows this, I think he's trying to throw me off and catch me in a lie.

"What's your homelife like?"

"My parents are out for themselves and I don't have much to do with them. I have two amazing grandparents and a sister who, by the way, is an avid Crushers' fan, has been since she first knew what hockey was."

"You trying to butter me up by telling me that?"

"Nope, just telling you about me and my family. Nanna and Pops are two of the most amazing and supportive people I know, I am who I am because of them."

Coach nods and then rapid fires question after question.

"Do you have any children?"

"No."

"Favorite color?"

"Black."

"Who buys your underwear, you, or your mom?"

"Ahh, me."

"What's the worst piece of advice either of your parents has ever given you?"

"You'll never make it as a hockey player, it's not a real career."

Chelsea reaches over and squeezes my knee. Coach doesn't bat an eyelid and continues to throw questions at me.

"Have you ever been arrested for DUI?"

Shaking my head, I reply, "Nope, never. Also, I've never had a speeding ticket."

"So, you drive like Miss Daisy then?"

"No, I drive according to the conditions and speed limits."

"Ever been to prison?"

Wanting to lighten the mood, I nod my head up and down. "Yes."

All three of them widen their eyes and their mouths drop open in shock.

"Explain," Coach demands.

"In senior year, I was incarcerated at Alcatraz for the day."

Coach's lips lift slightly and then he schools his expressions. "Very funny. Last question, what are your intentions with my daughter?"

"To make her happy and laugh and be the amazing person that she wants to be. I'll support her in anything she wants but most of all, when the time comes, I'll love her with every fiber of my being."

25
CHELSEA

Holy guacamole, who knew Kallen could be so sweet? Answering Daddy's questions like he did was like nothing I've ever seen before and then offering up bag skates, and Russian ones at that, as punishment if he screws me over is the sweetest thing ever. *He* would use me and our relationship to get out of drills like that, that should have been a warning sign, but I thought I was in love.

This time though, I'm going to keep my heart locked up tight until I'm one-billion-percent sure I'm ready to hand it over, but if Kallen keeps being all smooth and suave like this, that lock will easily disintegrate.

Dad stops with the twenty questions when the waitress arrives with our food. The four of us fall into easy conversation while we devour our brunch. Kal gives me a taste of his breakfast poutine and he can have that, it's totally not my thing.

One thing I've noticed this morning is, whenever Kal mentions his sister or grandparents his face lights up like a Christmas tree. It's almost as bright as when he and Dad talk about hockey.

Excusing myself, I make my way to the restrooms. While sitting on the toilet, a smile graces my face, odd place to grin, I know, but this morning could not have been better. It started with waking up in Kal's arms, yes, I headbutted him but that's neither here nor there. Then we joined Mom and Dad for brunch. To be honest, I was shit scared to come out to Dad, but thankfully, that went well, even with the twenty questions and him going all 'daddy protective' over me.

I'm on a high right now and nothing can bring me down.

Kal and I say goodbye to Mom and Dad and rather than heading straight back to his place, we go for a drive. We jump into his car and head over the Brooklyn Bridge, looking down as we reach the other side, I smile. "I love the carousel down there. Dad used to bring me over here every summer when I was little."

"Then let's do it now." Before I have a chance to reply, Kallen maneuvres his way through traffic, cutting a few people off at times.

After an eternity due to an accident on the express-way, and God knows how many missed turns and one-way streets, we park in a nearby garage that I found with Google. Hand in hand, we walk toward Jane's Carousel in Brooklyn Bridge Park.

The closer we get, the more excited I become. "I haven't been here in years," I tell him, as we line up to purchase tickets to ride it. I know it's a kids' thing but I'm a big kid at heart.

Finally, it's our turn and like an excited five-year-old, I race toward my favorite horse, it's on the inside and it's just as beautiful as I remember. Kal climbs onto the one next to mine. The music begins and we take off. Around and around we go.

Whipping out my phone, I take a selfie on my horse and snap a few candid shots of Kal before I yell out to him. He looks toward me, and I spin my back to him and take another selfie of the two of us.

Sooner than I'd like, our turn is over and we exit the carousel. We walk down to the river, where I lean on the rail and look out at the East River. Kal comes up behind me and presses his front to my back. "Thank you," he whispers into my ear.

Spinning around, I face him. "Why are you thanking me?"

"For taking a chance on me. This weekend has been amazing, and I hope to have many many more like this with you." I know it won't be weekends as such with the season starting, but any downtime I have I will be spending with Chels.

"Well, since we're offering gratitude, thank you for not giving up on me." I rest my head on his chest and cuddle him. He wraps his arms tight around me and there's no place I'd rather be. "I could have screwed us up, but you kept pushing me to take a leap and I'm so glad I did." Lifting up, I stare into his eyes and I see nothing but happiness staring back at me. "You, Kallen Jones, are an amazing man and I'm happy to officially be yours."

"Officially mine, I like that. Should we like cement this with a kiss?"

"That can be arranged." Lifting to my tippy-toes, I press my lips to his. Closing my eyes, I push my tongue into his mouth and kiss him with everything I have. Pulling back, I smile and bite my bottom lip. "That officially cements you as mine and me as yours."

"Maybe we need to cement it again, just to be sure."

"So demanding," I tease, "but I will happily oblige."

Kal slides his hand behind my head and pulls me into him. The kiss before was soft and sensual whereas this kiss is rough and frenzied.

"Chels, babe, if we don't stop kissing, I'm going to mount you right here in front of everyone. I don't think Coach or PR will be happy with the headline 'New Crushers' Goalie, Kallen Jones, Scores with His Coach's Daughter in Brooklyn' so I suggest we take this back to my place so I can show you in a more private way just how much you're mine."

"So thoughtful of you." I grab his hand in mine, "Let's go." I tug him away from the river and back toward the car.

Kal pulls me back into him and places a quick kiss on my lips before bending down and throwing me over this shoulder. He slaps me on the ass, and I let out a squeal that quickly turns into a moan when he rubs my ass cheek because his finger grazes between my thighs, turning me on more than I already am.

"Kal," I warn, "behave."

"I have no idea what you're referring to," he nonchalantly replies, but the butthead that he is, knows exactly what he's doing and to reiterate that thought, he slides his hand farther between my thighs. Hoping to give him some payback of my own, I grope his ass. My palms meet a muscular butt and when I squeeze, it seems to have no effect on him whatsoever. *Damn muscles.*

We reach his car, and he places me down on my feet beside the front passenger door. I stare up at him breathing heavily. "You, mister, are a big fat tease."

"It's not teasing if I promise to follow through on bringing you unimaginable pleasure."

"But your place is forever away and because of that stunt just now, I'm worked up and horny and just, gah."

He looks around the parking garage and I do too, seems we're the only ones here. He clicks the fob in his pocket and the car unlocks. Reaching behind me, he opens the door, but doesn't let me sit down. He looks me in the eyes and demands, "Undo your jeans, Chels, and sit on the edge of the seat facing me."

"Why?"

"Because I'm going to relieve that ache that's currently pulsating between your thighs."

"Here?" My eyes dart around the empty garage.

He nods. "Yes here, now hurry up or I'll make you wait 'til we get back to my place."

Feeling brave and adventurous, I swallow deeply,

take a deep breath, and with my eyes locked in his, I pop open the button on my jeans and lower the fly. Sliding my thumbs over the top of my jeans, I shimmy them down my thighs, thankful that I'm wearing my boyfriend-style jeans, so I can kick them off. Leaving me in my panties and tank.

"Faaaark, Chels, you are a vision."

"Now that you have me how you want me, what are you going to do?"

"This." He steps toward me. With one hand he cups my cheek in his palm and kisses me. With the other, he slides ever so slowly down my body. He cups my mound, his palm pressing against my clit and I moan into his kiss. He smiles against my lips. "You ready, babe?"

Nodding, I breathlessly wait. It feels like an eternity before I feel his hand move over the material of my thong, he pushes it to the side and runs his finger up and down my slit. "Yesssss," I mewl against his lips. That yes, turns into a garbled moan when he shoves his finger between my lips and inside.

Lifting my hands, I massage my breasts as he continues to thrust his finger in and out of me. My head drops back and I close my eyes, giving myself over to the pleasure building between my thighs. Kal licks up my neck, causing another wave of pleasure to build.

In the distance, a car engine roars to life and it's getting closer to us. Normally I'd be freaking the puck out, but right now, I'm lost to the bliss floating around my body. The car is in the row next to us and now I'm on edge.

"Kal," I plead, "someone's coming."

"Yes, you are."

"Kal," I groan, it's a mixture of protest and awe as he slips another finger in me.

"I'm not letting up 'til you come, Chels. So you better come right now, otherwise, that car is going to get an unobstructed view of my fingers plunging in and out of your pussy."

"I can't," I cry, panting as my orgasm draws closer.

"You can." And to show me that I can, his thumb presses on my clit and that's the detonation I need. Covering my mouth, I moan and explode all over his fingers. My body trembling as my orgasm ripples through my veins from head to toe.

Just as the car reaches us, Kal pushes me back into the car. Dropping to the seat with a thud, I shuffle back onto the seat and rest my head back against the headrest, trying to catch my breath. Kal drops down, picks up my jeans and drops them into my lap.

Leaning into me, he places a chaste kiss against my lips. "Told you you'd come." With a wink, he stands up and slams my door shut. Leaving me sitting here breathless to come down from my blissed-out state.

With a scoff I shake my head and grin, I'm so pucking screwed when it comes this man.

26
KALLEN

...four weeks later

Today is the first game of the season and my family is here to watch us hopefully beat the Toronto Gems. I can't wait to see them, it's just not the same via FaceTime but thankfully, I have Chelsea to keep me occupied in my downtime. She and I spend quite a bit of time together and we've been on some magical dates. I think my favorite was when we came back to the arena after dark one night, we entered via a back entrance that I never knew existed. Chels later let me know that she'd okayed access with her dad, the sound guy, and security. She told me to get my skates on and meet her in the tunnel to the ice.

With my skates on, I meet my girl and together, with our hands laced, we make our way to the rink. It's dark but there's a glow coming from the ice, giving off enough light to see where we are going without tripping over anything. When we step onto the ice, we skate into the middle and Chels yells, "Hit it." The lights flicker on, and it looks like millions of tiny stars flash above us. "I'm Yours" by Jason Mraz begins to play and she offers me her hand. Placing my hand in hers, we skate around. It's very romantic and Chels is amazing to skate with. "I never knew you could skate."

"Really? My dad is a hockey coach, I could skate before I could walk."

"Touché."

The song morphs into "Thunderstruck" by AC/DC. "Sorry." A feminine voice comes through the speaker system and the song skips to "You Belong with Me" by Taylor Swift.

"Is that Margot?" I ask Chels as we continue to skate around.

"Yep, I'm awesome but I couldn't have pulled this off by myself."

Pulling her into my arms, I stare deep into her soul. "Thank you, this is amazing." Leaning forward, I press my lips to her.

"Get a room you two," Margot teases as Chels and I both laugh.

"You can leave now!" Chels shouts at her friend.

"Peace out peoples. Don't do anything I wouldn't do," she coos through the speakers.

"That doesn't leave us much," she informs me.

"Lucky us then." I raise my eyebrows at her.

"Fiend." She slaps my chest.

"Only for you, baby." Cupping her cheeks, I slam my

lips to hers and then we continue to skate around for an evening that will be embedded in my mind forever. I will never forget it.

Sitting in front of my stall, I stare at the two photos I have stuck up, my family and Chels and me from our evening here. I love that we don't have to hide our relationship. After coming out to Coach, we had to come out to the team. I think I was more worried about that and that they'd be antsy about me dating the coach's daughter, but they've all been great about it. Well, almost everyone.

Doucheman is living up to his name and being a right royal douche but Coach and Anton don't take his shit. I think in the last six weeks, he's done more bag skates than I have in my entire life but he deserves it, especially after what he pulled two weeks ago at practice...

...after this drill, we're done for the day." Coach is giving us a half day so we can go home and prepare for tomorrow's charity event. This event has been in the works for months. It's to raise money for the program that Doc Michels is working on to aid in sports recovery. To say I'm nervous would be an understatement because many of the attendees are previous players, who have been idols of mine from when they were playing, and to be hanging with them and my fans, it's surreal. My fans, it's so weird saying that.

My rest tonight however will involve me balls deep inside Chels, followed by a hearty meal, and then I'll fall into bed with Chelsea wrapped in my arms, my new favorite way to sleep. Whether we're at her place or mine, I don't care. As long as she's in my arms, that's all I need to have a full night's sleep.

Coach has everyone lined up at the other end of the rink, they skate toward me in pairs and it's my job to block the shot when they crash the crease. And along the way, they will each hone their skills on the ice.

Jett and Anton are up first, they leisurely shoot the puck back and forth. The rest of the team chirps me. Anton breaks away and takes the shot, the puck safely landing in my pad. "Next time, Cap. Next time," I tease him as he skates on by.

JJ and Däuchmen are up next. JJ is pissed that he's teamed with Däuchmen and his anger increases when Däuchmen doesn't pass the puck to him once. He makes his way down the ice, coming straight at me, he fakes to the left and takes the shot. The puck slides between my legs and into the goal. "Dammit," I mumble to myself.

Däuchmen cheers as if he's King Ding-a-ling. "You suck, Jones," he chortles as the coach growls his name, earning himself a talking-to from Coach for not passing the puck. Coach makes him and JJ repeat the drill. This time he passes the puck back and forth to JJ, once again he takes the shot but this time, it hits the crossbar, not going in. He's pissed he missed the shot but skates back down to the next team and waits for his next turn.

So far today, I've only missed three shots. This is the last run for today's session, and the last two to come at me are JJ and Däuchmen. On their second run, they worked effortlessly together, and JJ managed to sneak the puck into the goal, so I'm out to win this time around. Like last round, the two of them pass the puck back and forth, and I skate out of the crease for something differ-ent. Däuchmen passes to JJ at the last second and some-thing passes over his face. He puts some oomph into his skating, and he makes a beeline for me. I think he's going to go around me and have JJ pass to him, but the asshole lowers his shoulder, and he slams into me at speed. The force pushes us both backward and my back collides with the goal crossbar. I go down like a sack of potatoes with the wind knocked out of me. I see stars when I collapse to the ice. I can hear yelling around me, but everything is muffled as I blink rapidly, clearing my vision.

Finally, my vision clears and I see one of the trainers above me, his lips are moving but no sound is registering right now. All I can focus on is the pain in my back, which is currently radiating down my left leg.

Closing my eyes for a few moments, I take a few deep breaths and when I open them again, Anton and JJ are above me with the trainer. "You okay, dude?" I'm not sure which one of them said that because everything is still muffled.

"That was a massive hit you just took," the trainer says, concern etched all over his face.

"No shit, but did I stop the puck?" I ask, grinning to myself.

"Fuck the puck," JJ spits, shaking his head. "You okay? Can you wiggle your toes?"

"Wiggle my toes, really?"

"I don't know what to ask, I've never seen anyone take a hit like that before, not up close. Even I flinched when you hit the ice."

"I did more than flinch," I tell him, "and when I get back on my feet, Doucheman is a dead doucheman."

"At least your sense of humor is still intact," Anton jokes. "But right now, Coach is ripping him a new one for the 'accident' just now." He air quotes accident. "I have a feeling that he'll be bag skating it for the foreseeable future."

"And become acquainted with my fist."

"Easy there, Rocky Balboa. Let's get you off the ice and get Doc Michels to have a look at you. Lucky for you, Lexi is also here working on their sports injury thingy. I'm sure she'll work her magic fingers on you." Lexi Knight, is our physical therapist, who at the moment is working alongside Dr. Michels with his sports rehab program for elite athletes. She's hot, not as hot as my Chelsea, but apart from being hot, she's one amazing physical therapist. I also think there's history between her and JJ because you can cut the tension between the two of them with a knife.

Nodding, the guys help me up and when I'm back on my feet, the rest of the team claps in relief when they see me upright. Coach leaves a pissed-off-looking Doucheman and comes over to me.

"You okay, Jones?"

"Nothing an ice bath won't fix."

"I want Doc to give you a once over before you leave and without their clearance, you won't be attending tomorrow's charity event."

"But, Coach—"

"No buts, Jones. No clearance. No play."

"Yes, Coach," I sullenly reply, wincing in pain when I huff in frustration.

With the assistance of JJ and Anton, they slowly help me back to the locker room. Removing all my gear, I'm grunting and groaning, my muscles pulling as I strip off. Grabbing my towel, I stand up and walk, well shuffle, toward the shower. Reaching in, I turn the water on. Once it's hot, I step in under the spray and let out a groan when the hot water hits my skin. It hurts too much to move, so I lower my head, stand under the showerhead and let the water do its thing.

"You okay in there?" Anton asks me.

"Yeah," I reply, "I'll be out in a sec." Turning the faucet off, I grab my towel and dry off, wincing when I bend down to dry my legs. Wrapping my towel around my waist, I head over to Doc's office, but he isn't there. Poking my head into the next room, I see Lexi sitting at her desk in her treatment room.

Knocking on the door, she looks up and her eyes widen when she sees me standing here in just my towel. "Can you have a look at my back, I had a fall during practice."

"A fall," JJ snarls from the other side of the locker room, "more like you were plowed into by a raging asshole."

"I wouldn't say plowed," I refute.

"Ohh, I'm sorry," he scoffs, "how else do you describe Doucheman hitting you at full speed and Kronwalling you into the goal?"

"Well, yeah, technically that's what happened—"

"Not technically, actually," JJ spits as he joins me in the doorway, his eyes roaming over my body. He shakes his head at the already forming bruise that's wrapping from my back around to my abdomen. "Doucheman is a real

fucking douche for doing that. This better not fuck up your season."

"I'm fine," I growl at him through clenched teeth, but his words echo in my mind because I think he might have done some damage.

"JJ, out, I need to call Doc so he and I can assess Jones and I can't do that with you being you, so out." She walks over to us. She pulls me into the room and glares at JJ. "Go on, scoot." He takes a step back and she slams the door in his face. She looks at me and head nods toward the table. Carefully I sit on the edge as she calls Doc. "Doc's on his way but while we wait, talk to me, Jones, where does it hurt?"

"My back."

She nods. "Can you lift your arms so I can have a look at your movements?"

Nodding, I lift my arm over my head, wincing the higher I raise it up. It pulls at the muscles in my back and I flinch.

"Holy shit," she whispers, gently running her fingertip over my back just as there's a knock on the door and Doc walks in. Lexi confers with Doc and I sit here, awaiting my fate.

Doc walks over to me. "Kallen, can you lie face down so I can have a feel around?"

"Sure." I shuffle onto my stomach, and he gets to it. I gasp and wince a few times but all in all, I don't feel too bad.

"Nothing seems to be broken, but we'll get an X-ray to be sure. I also want you to have an ice bath now to help with the muscle aches. You have a hot tub at home?"

"Yep," I yelp, the spot he just hit tender under his gentle touch.

"Good," he states.

Turning my head to face him, I see him nodding and Lexi biting her lip. Her index finger taps her chin as she thinks. Lexi is the best physical therapist and masseuse around so with her and Doc looking after me, I know I'm in good hands. "I want you to take a few maintenance days. When you're back, come and see me and Lexi each day until we clear you. We will make sure you're healing nicely."

"But the charity thing is tomorrow."

"Do you want to be ready for the opener? Or do you want to attend a charity thing that's possibly going to set you back?"

"Both," I grumble.

"Well, you can't do both," Lexi snaps, that's one thing we all love about Lexi. She may look like this cute wee woman but she's tough as nails. She gives as good as she gets and she doesn't take our crap, and right now with her and Doc assessing me, I'm glad they're mine, well the Crushers'. "After your ice bath, come back and see me. I'll rub arnica using this new technique I read about into the area to bring out any bruising and start the healing process."

"That's a great idea, Lexi, make sure to document everything so we can refer back to it for future reference."

She nods at Doc and then turns her attention back to me. "Tomorrow we'll repeat what I do tonight."

"Won't that hurt?"

"Do you want to play the first game of the season?"

"Yes," I quickly reply.

"Then suck it up and let my hands work their magic."
She waves her fingers at me with a 'let me do my job' look
on her face.

"Did anyone ever tell you, you're a sadist?"

An evil smile appears on her face. "Only you big tough
hockey boys when you have a boo-boo."

Doc laughs and exits Lexi's treatment room.

Shaking my head, Lexi and I exit the room and she
begins getting my ice bath ready. Climbing into the ice
tub, I groan at the chill and I swear, my balls shrivel and
head inward.

Lying back, I close my eyes and let the ice do its job
before Lexi tortures me with her magic cream and hands...

..."You good to go, Jones?" Lexi asks, snapping me
back to the present. Her eyes flicking over my body,
assessing me.

Nodding, I grin at her. "Of course I am, I have the
best doc and massage slash physical therapist on speed
dial."

She rolls her eyes at me. "Don't make me regret
giving you my number."

"How come you gave him your number but not me?"
JJ whines from next to me.

"Because he needed my help."

"What if I need your help?"

"I'm sure Doc Michels will be on hand to help with
anything you need," she growls at him, turns on her heel,
and walks back to her room. Before she steps inside, she
looks over her shoulder at JJ and me. "And, guys, good

luck out there today." Her gaze lingers on JJ for a few seconds before she closes the door behind her.

"What's going on between you two?" I ask JJ.

"Nothing," he snaps, but blind Freddie can see that something is going on between them. I raise my eyebrows at him in that 'do I look dumb' way. He lets out a sigh, "Dude, seriously *nothing* is happening." He places emphasis on the word nothing, reaffirming that something has happened in the past and now it's a nothing, but he doesn't want it to be a nothing. Dammit, I'm turning into my sister with all this gossiping, even if it is with myself internally.

"But you want there to be?"

"Dude, I've been in love with that girl since senior year at school…"

"But?"

"I fucked it all up."

"What happened?"

"Long story and we have our debut game to focus on." He turns his back on me and starts to get ready, officially ending our conversation, but he's left me intrigued as to what happened between the two of them.

It must be because my love life is going well, I walk over to him and squeeze his shoulder. "Maybe this is your chance to win her back."

"Maybe," he dejectedly sighs.

Walking back to my stall, I start to pull my pads on.

It's showtime, Kallen Jones is about to make his debut in the NHL, puck yeah, baby!

27

KALLEN

"My grandson, the professional hockey player," Nanna coos when I meet up with her, Pops, and Kendall outside the family lounge after our win against the Gems. She throws her arms around my waist for a Nanna hug and I slightly wince. Even though I'm mostly healed, I'm still not one hundred percent after my run-in with Doucheman the other week. Add to that the muscle aches from training in general and tonight's game and I'm a little tender to the touch right now. I might need to see if Nurse Chelsea is available for a home visit later tonight.

Speaking of Chelsea, the minx that she is, bought a sexy nurse's outfit and played naughty nurse for me. She has extraordinary skills in the medical field, well, with her mouth anyway. Due to my injuries, she wouldn't have sex with me, but she did allow me to fuck her tits again and each night ended with a blow job before she tucked me in and went home. I did *not* like waking up alone for that week, but she assured me it was for my health.

I'm snapped back to the present from Sexy Nurse-town when Pops pulls me in for a hug. He steps back and my sister jumps into my arms, hugging the life out of me, I manage to wrap my arms around her and hide the tenderness from her embrace. "You are an asset to my team, Kal, but don't fuck it up 'cause I'd hate to have to kill you," she whispers the swear words because Nanna would tan her ass if she heard her angel, Kendall, using language like that.

"Thanks, Sis," I reply. "It's nice to know you love the team more than my life."

She shrugs at me and before I can throw back a retort, a voice that is like fingernails down a chalkboard inter-rupts us. "Cheating on her already...and in the hallway where she can walk in anytime," Doucheman chortles. "You've got balls of steel, Jones. I'm kinda impressed." He comes to a stop next to us and I turn to face him, but his eyes are steadfastly locked on Kendall in a creepy way. I notice she has taken a step back away from us. His eyes light up in a predatory way the longer he ogles my sister. "Babycakes, when you tire of him," he flicks his thumb in my direction, "come see me."

Kendall stares at him and from the expression on her face, I just know that Doucheman is going to get it and I can't wait to see this play out. She steps into his personal space, over her shoulder he gives me a smarmy look, that is until Kendall grabs his chin in her grip, no doubt squeezing in the way that causes pain—my sister is evil like that. "I wouldn't touch you if you were the last man alive and us procreating was the only thing to save humanity. Do us all a favor and fuck off." She looks over her shoulder to Nanna. "Sorry, Nanna." But from the look on Nanna's face, she doesn't mind the swear this time around. Kendall turns her attention back to Doucheman, "Now run along, Doucheman,"—she places emphasis on the douche part of doucheman—"you're not wanted here."

"Fu—" he goes to reply but Pops steps toward him and squeezes his shoulder.

"You heard her, you're not wanted here, boy. Now run along before I let her at you again."

Doucheman's eyes widen and with his tail between his legs, he shuffles away, mumbling under his breath about disrespect and getting what's coming. The four of us watch as he marches away, shoulder-barging into anyone in his way. Shaking my head, I continue to watch him throw his temper tantrum all the way to the exit. I'm thankful that Chels wasn't here to witness him just now. He seriously is unhinged and trouble.

"That boy's trouble," Nanna voices my thought and I smile at her. "If he was my grandson, I'd paddle his ass with his hockey stick."

"You and me both, hon." Pops agrees with Nanna, pulling her protectively into his side.

"Your family is totally badass," JJ says from behind me, I hadn't even realized he'd joined us. He walks around me and over to Nanna. "How are you, Nanna?" He greets her before pulling her away from Pops and wrapping his arms around her in a bear hug, spinning her around.

Nanna giggles and when he places her back down on her feet, she cups his cheek in her palm. "Jameson, how are you?" She looks lovingly up at him in that proud Nanna way she does. JJ and Nanna became close when he and I roomed together at college. He'd always interrupt my FaceTime calls and by the third week, he was FaceTiming her without me.

"I'm good. On a pucking high after tonight's game, thanks to our boy here." He throws his arm around my shoulder, pulls me down, and ruffles my hair. "Saving puck after puck."

"He sure played well." Nanna looks to me and then cups my cheek like she just did to JJ. "I'm so proud of you, Kallen."

"Thanks, Nanna." Reaching up, I squeeze her hand on my cheek but quickly drop it when I hear my name being yelled from behind me. Turning around, I smile when I see Chelsea and Nessa walking into the lounge. Chelsea breaks out into a sprint and when she's a few feet in front of me, she leaps at me. My arms wrap around her and I spin us around. "You were amazing out there," she excitedly cheers. Lowering her head, she covers my mouth with hers for an all-consuming kiss.

Cat calls and wolf whistles echo through the room. I put Chelsea back down on her feet. "That was quite the hello."

"Only the best for the best goalie in the NHL."

"Not sure about that. Let's settle for best boyfriend in the NHL."

"That too," she agrees. "Can't wait 'til we can celebrate just the two of us." She leans in. "I may have purchased a sexy cheerleader outfit for tonight."

"Babe, you can't tell me that when I can't get you alone for a few more hours yet."

"Also, just so you know," she leans in closer, her breath heating my skin. "I'm not wearing any underwear under this." She steps back and raises her eyebrows suggestively at me. My eyes rake over my sexy as puck girlfriend and my cock twitches in my dress pants. She's wearing black leather pants that look like they're painted on and a Crushers' jersey, when she turns around to greet Nanna and Pops, I see my number and name reflecting back at me.

"It's official now," JJ says, clapping me on the back, "she's wearing *your* jersey, you don't get more official than that."

He's right, you don't get more official than that and I could not be happier. We won our first game of the season. My girl is wearing my jersey and right now, she and Nanna are chatting away as if they've known each other for years. This is the first time they've met in person and seeing them get along like this warms my heart. How did I get so lucky to land my dream job and dream girl?

28

CHELSEA

Tʜɪs ᴘʀᴇss ᴛʜɪɴɢ ᴀꜰᴛᴇʀ ᴛᴏɴɪɢʜᴛ's sᴇᴀsᴏɴ ᴏᴘᴇɴᴇʀ home game win is dragging on and on, I much prefer when they do it straight after the game but there was some breaking news thing and it was delayed. Reporters ask the same question fifty different ways, but tonight I don't mind so much because I'm focused on my sexier than puck boyfriend. He was amazing out there tonight and the Crushers, if they play like they did tonight every game, have a real shot at bringing home the Cup this season.

"You really are taken with him, aren't you?" Mom asks from beside me, gently nudging me.

Nodding, I smile when I turn to face her. "Yeah, I really am, Mom. He's nothing like *him* and I'm so glad I gave Kal a chance."

"Never let a man dictate your life. Yes, Stefan hurt you in an unimaginable way and one day karma will get him, but it's made you a stronger person because of it and I'm so proud of you."

"Why are you proud?"

"Because you got over your fear and have opened your heart up to love again. Chels, you deserve all the happiness in the world and that man up there," she points to the front of the room where the team and Daddy are sitting right now, "hasn't been able to take his eyes off you since they landed on you when we arrived. In the few weeks you have been with him, I've seen you blossom. I can't remember the last time I saw you smiling so much."

"He makes me happy, Mom, in a way I've never felt before."

"Sounds like love to me."

"It can't be love, it's too soon."

"When you know, you know. I knew I loved your father from the moment I laid eyes on him, and I love him just as much today as I did back then. Sure, there are days I want to smother him with a pillow, especially when it comes to his clothes and them not making it into the laundry hamper, but at the end of the day, it's those things that also make me love him."

"Just like he hates that you have to unpack the groceries 'cause we all do it wrong, but then you whine that no one helps you."

"Exactly."

"Or that we hang out the laundry wrong and fold things the incorrect way or—"

"Okay, I get it, I'm quirky."

"And we wouldn't have you any other way, Mom. Not sure it's love with Kallen, but I can definitely see a future with him. I'm going to take one day at a time, and for now, I'll keep the current goalie protecting my heart." Mom raises her eyebrows at my analogy. "Not that goalie," I point to the front of the room, "this goalie," I tap my chest, "me."

"Whatever you say, but I think whichever goalie you're referring to makes you a lucky gal."

Nodding, I bite my bottom lip and process Mom's words about my heart and which goalie I'm referring to in protecting it. I think she might be right in that it's Kallen. In the few short weeks we've been together, I'm happier than I have ever been before. He's bringing out my sexually adventurous side—hello, I own a slutty nurse and sexy cheerleader outfit—but most of all, he makes me smile, even when he's not around and he accepts me for me, Chelsea, not Chelsea, Coach Maxwell's daughter.

Hands slide around my waist from behind. Closing my eyes, I lean back into him and rest my hands on his arms hugging me. "What's got you so happy?" He breathes into my ear, causing goose pimples to erupt on my skin.

"A lot of things," I inform him.

"A lot, like what?"

Spinning around in his arms, I drape mine over his shoulders and stare into his bluer than blue eyes. "Well, for starters, my team won their opening game tonight because their amazing goalie was on fire, and I'm about to head out for a fantabulous dinner with my family and friends."

"Is that all?" he pushes.

"Ohh, and I'm dating this hotter than hot guy. I'm waiting for him to kiss me because it's been far too long since I've had his lips on mine."

"Well, we can't have that now, can we?"

"No, we can't." I look at him in a seductive way that somehow has *my* body buzzing.

"I should go and find this guy and kick his ass," Kal teases, staring intently at me. The intensity of his gaze causes the inferno already raging inside of me to intensify.

"You could, or you could just kiss me, maybe make him jealous." Shrugging at him, I bite my lip and wait in anticipation for his lips to be pressed against mine.

"I'm sure I can do that, and for the record," he pulls me closer to him, "I better be the only guy you're kissing." Before I can confirm he's the only one, he slams his lips to mine. He slips his tongue into my mouth, sweeping it around, leaving me breathless and heady.

"Jealous much?"

"I'm jealous of the fact that your clothes are touching the parts that I want to be touching and pissed that I have a dinner to attend before I can touch said parts."

"Who said you can't do both?" Pulling back, I wink at him and walk over to Mom, Dad, his sister, Nanna, and Pops.

As I walk away from him, I realize that Mom's right, I do love him. But for now, I'll keep it to myself because I don't think I will be able to handle another heartbreak.

"Can we get out of here yet?" Kal whines for the millionth time.

"Not yet, you big baby." I tap his cheek. "This is tradition for the Crushers after the first game of the season and I will not have you messing with tradition and the team."

"You sound like my sister, I just need you to add, 'don't fuck my team up' and it will be like talking to her."

"Well, they aren't *my* team so I won't be saying that. Speaking of your sister, where is she?"

"She and Nanna are pressing Anton for gossip."

"But he's the least gossipy person on the team."

"You and I know that; Nanna and Kendall don't know that."

"Should we go rescue him?" I ask Kal, staring over at an awkward-looking Anton and Kal's excited Nanna and sister."

"Nah, let them have their fun."

I state the obvious, "Anton's not having fun."

"Meh, he made me do an extra set in the gym the other day, this is payback for that."

"You know karma will bite you in the ass for being petty like that."

"Maybe...but I'd much rather bite your ass."

"That's a maybe," I cheekily tell him.

"Really?"

"Maybe."

"You continue to surprise me, Chelsea Maxwell."

"Just keeping you on your toes, Kallen Jones."

We stare at one another, the air around us crackling with desire, that is until *he* barges between us, snapping us away from our moment. "Get a room," Stefan snarls, dropping his shoulder into Kal.

"Really, Stefan?" I scold him.

"Really what?" he snaps, turning toward me. His face full of rage and anger, nothing like the Stefan I used to know. Then he looks to Kal and if looks could kill, Kal would be six feet under right now. "Don't you think it's poor taste to hook up with one of your teammates exes?"

"Don't you think it's poor taste to fuck three puck bunnies while you were dating Chels?" Kal throws back at him.

"She could have joined in but nooooo, she—"

"Stefan," I beg, trying to diffuse the situation, but I'm not doing a very good job. I can feel everyone's eyes on me, but I cannot focus on them now, I need to focus on fixing this. "Please don't do this."

"Do what?" he growls, spittle flying from his mouth. "State the truth, that you're a frigid bitch who had to rat me out to Daddy 'cause she can't handle a real man... must be why she's with you, Jones. She went from this," he flicks his hands up and down his body, "to that," he points at Kal and shakes his head. He steps closer to Kal and pokes him in the chest. "Watch her, she'll fuck you over like she fucked me over." He pauses and then tacks on, "Make sure you lock in that deal first."

With that, he shoulder-barges Kal and storms away

from us. That's when I notice the silence. When I look around the room, I see that all eyes are on us. "You okay?" Kal rubs my arm in that caring Kal way.

Nodding that I'm okay, I swallow down the lump in the back of my throat, but I'm far from okay. From the corner of my eye, I see Mom and Dad walking over to us, but I can't deal with them right now, I need space. "Excuse me," I tearfully mumble and I race out of the room. With each step I take toward the exit, I can feel everyone's eyes on me, and I hate being the center of attention.

Racing down the hallway, I enter the restrooms and dive into a stall. Closing the door behind me, I lock it and sit down. Leaning my elbows on my knees, I cover my face with my hands. The first tear falls and before I know it, I'm a sobbing mess. I let it all out but the sadness soon turns to anger. How dare *he* say that to Kal and me? He was the one to puck up, not me.

"Chels, you in here?" an unfamiliar voice says from the doorway. Not wanting to talk to anyone yet, I remain quiet but my body decides that I need company and out of nowhere, I sneeze...four times in a row.

"Bless you. Bless you. Bless you. Bless you," comes the voice from the other side of the door.

"Thank you," I automatically reply.

"You wanna come out and talk to me?" they ask me.

"No," I quietly reply.

"Well, if you don't talk to me, I'll be forced to get my brother, who is pacing the corridor worried about his girlfriend."

Kendall, I think to myself and then I focus on her

words, Kal is worried. For some reason that makes me smile. Lifting my hand, I unlock the door but I make no move to exit the safety of the stall.

The door creaks open and Kendall pops her head through the crack. "You okay?"

"Not really," I honestly tell her, shaking my head side to side. "Just when I think everything is fine with *him*, he shows his true colors and I'm back to square one again."

"Best thing you can do is not let that douche affect you. Pretend Stefan Däuchmen doesn't exist and focus on you and what you want, which I have a feeling just so happens to be my brother."

"But how do I do that when I see *him* every day at work and he's Kal's teammate?"

"Ignore him. When you see him, pretend he's not there. When you retaliate, he wins, and a douche like him doesn't deserve to win. Trust me, a narcissist like him will be pissed that he isn't getting to you."

"How can you be so sure?"

"I'm not sure, but I've never seen my brother so happy and smitten before. I'll do anything for my baby bro to be happy, anything. If I could, I'd kick Däuchmen's ass and get him off the team, but I don't have those powers. Hell, not even your dad can get rid of him and he's the coach."

"Daddy tried so hard to get rid of him last season, but his contract is locked up tight."

"But his contract is up at the end of this season, it's just a matter of time. We just have to patiently wait until Stefan Däuchmen is no longer a Crusher...maybe the

Vikings will take him." She shudders as the word Vikings passes through her lips.

"I would have thought being from Vancouver, you'd be a Vikings fan."

"Everyone thinks that but I've always loved the Crushers, I think 'cause purple is my favorite color and when I was little, purple was everything to me." She laughs. "I remember when I was like five, I only ever ate purple foods.

A laugh escapes me and I smile up at her. "Thank you, Kendall."

"You're welcome, now, come and see my brother before he breaks this door down and we have to bail him out of jail for damaging public property."

Standing up, I walk to the sink and stare at my reflection. I look like a hot mess right now, but what's new with me? I need to go find my man and reassure him I'm fine.

29

KALLEN

S<small>EEING THE HURT ON</small> C<small>HELSEA'S FACE JUST ABOUT</small> broke me. If Doucheman was still here, his face would become acquainted with my fist. "He's such a douche," Kendall says joining me, then she adds, "and if you don't go after her, you are just as much of a douche."

Her words spark me into action and I exit the room, looking left I don't see her but when I turn my head toward the main restaurant, I see her enter the restroom. "Shit," I snap and I race down the hallway. Coming to a stop, I stare at the closed door before me.

"What's wrong?" Kendall asks, joining me.

"She went into the restroom."

"So?" she throws back at me, looking confused.

"She went into the ladies' restroom."

"So?" she sasses again.

"Ladies' restroom." Emphasizing the word ladies, I

turn my back on her and begin to pace back and forth, contemplating if I should barge in there myself.

She shakes her head, and smirks at me. "You're such a goody-goody. I'll go get her."

"Thank you." I nod at my sister. She turns around and enters the restroom. I continue to pace back and forth in front of the closed door like a total creeper, waiting for it to open.

After what feels like a billion years, the door moves but I deflate when I see Kendall. "She'll be out in a moment."

"Thanks, Sis." I smile at her but keep my eye on the door behind her.

"Anytime." She shoulder-bumps me and then walks back to the room where the dinner is being held. After what again feels like another billion years, the door opens and standing before me is a sad and aloof looking Chelsea.

"Chels," I voice, stepping over to her, "you okay?" Stretching out my hand, she stares at it for a few beats before she places hers in mine. My hand dwarfs her dainty one but somehow, they fit together perfectly.

"I'm fine," she quietly utters. "Just..." She drops her gaze and stares at the carpet below.

"Just what? Talk to me, beautiful."

She lifts her gaze to mine. "I'm just sick of *him* ruining everything."

"He hasn't ruined shit, well, his reputation is ruined but nothing he does ruins anything for me or for us." Realizing we are standing outside the restrooms; I walk us toward an alcove just near the main restaurant.

"How are you so okay with this?"

"Because he's nothing to me," I state matter-of-factly. "If I don't let him bother me, there's nothing to worry about and he becomes moot. Plus, a bonus of my nonchalance is it pisses him off. I don't have to lift a finger to do that, so it's win/win."

She wraps her arms around my waist and rests her head on my chest. "Thank you for everything."

"You never need to thank me. I'm here for you, Chels. The good. The bad. The ugly and most of all, for the sexy tequila naked times."

She laughs and slaps me on the chest. "Stop, you can't say that to me when we have to go back into the dinner. I'm not wearing any underwear under these pants, and I don't want sexy schmexy to run down my leg while in the same room as my mom and dad...or your grandparents."

"Well, you shouldn't be such a minx and wear underwear."

"VPL," she replies with a shrug.

"What VPL?"

"Visible Panty Line. These pants are painted on." She pulls away from me, turns around, lifts up her—my—jersey and thrusts her ass at me. "I don't want panty lines ruining my look."

"Babe, as much as it pains me to say this, put your ass away, otherwise, I'm going to walk back into that room with a boner."

With her sexy as hell ass still pointing at me, she huskily murmurs, "We can always," she head nods toward the restrooms, "and I can fix that."

"As tempting, and gross, as that is, we need to get back before your dad comes in search of you. It's one thing to be dating the coach's daughter, it's another to get caught fucking in public."

"Spoilsport," she teases and then she looks at me seriously. "As soon as this thing is over, we need to get some tequila, get back to your place, and get naked."

"Dammit, Chelsea, looks like I'm walking back in with a boner."

"Ohh, you called me Chelsea, I must be in trouble." She bites her bottom lip. "Come on, let's get back in there so we can get this thing over with and then we can get out of here."

"Give me a minute." She looks questioningly at me, I lower my gaze to my cock, currently tenting my pants.

"Did I do that?" she playfully teases.

"No, it's the guy at the table over there." She looks over her shoulder and then bursts out laughing. I find myself laughing too because the guy I'm referring to must weigh at least three hundred pounds, has sweat stains all over his was once white shirt, and his belly almost reaches his feet while he's sitting down.

Our laughs garner his attention and for some reason, this makes us laugh harder, and thankfully deflates my cock. Linking my arm with hers, we walk back toward the private room. When we enter, Nessa is the first to envelop her daughter into a mom hug. She pulls back and grips Chels's cheeks. "You okay?"

"I am now, thanks to Kendall and Kal."

Nessa looks to me and smiles and then pulls me in for a mom hug. "Thank you for looking after my little girl."

"Always," I reply.

Coach clears his throat. "I'm sorry I can't kick his sorry ass off the team, Pumpkin."

"I know, Daddy, and you don't need to worry or protect me. I'm a big girl, Dad, I can fight my own battles."

"I know, Pumpkin, but it's my prerogative as a father to protect you. Always."

"And mine too," I add.

"And I thank you both but as I said, I'm a big girl. I'm happy, finally, and I'm not going to let *him* ruin that. His words are just that, words. By ignoring him, I win and one of these days, he'll either get what he deserves, or he'll realize that he has no hold over me and move on."

"You, my beautiful, amazing daughter are phenomenal." Coach is staring at his daughter with nothing but love for her etched on his face.

"'Cause I have an amazing dad." A throat clears and we all look to Nessa, who is watching on with a smile of adoration on her face but also a look that says 'Hey, what about me?' "And a fantabulous mom," she tacks on. Pulling away from Coach, she walks over to her mom and wraps her arms around Nessa again. Nessa hugs her daughter back tightly, and the scene between the two of them is just beautiful.

The two of them are whispering and I think it might be about me because they each look over at me. Shyly I smile and then Chels pulls away from Nessa and walks over to me. She looks into my eyes and I feel her gaze deep in my soul. "I meant what I said to Daddy, you've given me what I need to deal with *him*. He's here and there's not anything we can do about it, but *we* can control how we react to *him*. Ignoring his taunts and forgetting that Stefan Däuchmen exists is how I'm going to move forward. Now, let's get out of here." She winks seductively at me and my cock is once again, semi hard. This woman is going to be the pucking death of me.

30
CHELSEA

THE LAST FEW WEEKS WITH KAL AND THE TEAM HAS been amazing—even with *him*. I took my own advice and have been ignoring him. I've been ignoring his taunts, his suggestions that Kal is using me, and his 'you'll be begging me to take you back' rants. It's pathetic how he's trying to paint Kal as the bad guy when in actual fact *he* is the baddest of them all.

Janice returned to work three weeks ago, and I stayed on as the team's official social media guru. Jackie in marketing was impressed with what I was doing while I was helping Dad out—I started to blog and document what the team was up to behind the scenes. They were impressed and offered me an official position with the marketing team. It was great to be hired for something that I did and not because I'm David Maxwell's daughter.

The team has just returned from a week of away

games and to say I'm exhausted is an understatement, I swear my job is harder when they're away than when they're home. "I'm exhausted," I whine, flopping down onto Kal's couch. "I think this blogging job is harder than being Dad's executive assistant."

Removing my shoes, I shuffle back into the cushions, close my eyes, and drape my arm over my forehead. I could quite easily fall asleep right now, but we need to eat, and I really should head home and prepare for the week ahead.

"Me too," he agrees from behind me. "And I'm famished." No sooner has he finished that statement than I feel him at my feet. Opening my eyes, I look down and I'm met with the hungry sexy stare of Kallen Jones—he's famished for me, not for food. My panties immediately soak—a common occurrence around Kal—at the carnal look on his face.

Skimming his hands up my legs, he grips the waistband of my leggings and begins to pull them and my panties down. Lifting up, I give him room to remove them completely. Leaving me in nothing but my bra and Crushers' tank. "You look fucking edible," he growls. The deep timbre of his voice vibrates through my body.

We silently stare at one another. My heart rate increases as I wait for him to make his move. This is sexual torture of the best kind and I know that the wait will be worth it. I raise my eyebrows in a 'what are you waiting for' way and quicker than *The Flash*, my legs are spread wide, and his tongue is licking between my folds.

"Kaaaaaal," I moan, gripping my breasts as he licks, sucks, and devours me with his tongue. Closing my eyes, I give myself over to the pleasure building within. I'm on the cusp of coming when suddenly he stops. My eyes open and I'm ready to stare daggers at him, that is until I see him removing his pants and sheathing his rock-hard cock with a condom. He surprises me by dropping back to his knees and resuming to lick and suck me.

A few licks later and I'm ready to detonate, "I'm cooooommmmmmming," I squeal as I explode all over his face. Wave after wave of orgasmic pleasure trembles throughout my body. I'm still riding my orgasmic high when he lines himself up at my entrance and thrusts himself inside of me.

That high quickly kicks back into gear and I'm once again working my way up to orgasm number two. This man is going to be the death of me and my vagina but right now, I don't pucking care. I just need to come and I'm so close.

"Come for me, baby," Kal demands. "Come all over my cock."

Hmmm, this is different. He's never dirty talked like this before and I think I like it.

"I'm close," he growls through clenched teeth. "I'm not coming until you do, so you need to come now, Chels."

As if his words have a direct line to my pussy, I explode all over his dick. I come harder than I ever have before and it sets him off. Kal's body above me tenses and he explodes, grunting through his release.

When he's finished, he flips us around so I'm now lying on top of him. I close my eyes and rest my head on his chest. When my breathing is back under control, I lift my head and stare down at him. "That was unexpected."

"What was?"

"The dirty talk. I...I liked it."

"Duly noted." He lifts his head and places a kiss on my lips. "Now that I've had my appetizer, we should get cleaned up so I can have my main dish."

"And what's on the menu for tonight?" Even though I've just come twice, I'm hoping he says me.

"I'm thinking steak."

"Ohh," I dejectedly reply.

"With you for dessert," he tacks on.

Smiling up at him, I nod. "And maybe I can have you as a nightcap?"

"I'm sure that can be arranged."

And that's exactly what we do. Kallen and I order in an amazing steak meal—thank you, DoorDash—he has me for dessert...on the dining table and I have him as a nightcap before we drift off to sleep in each other's arms.

The night and my life are perfect at the moment, things are finally looking up for me, and for once, I'm not pucking screwed. I'm pucking over the moon happy.

31
KALLEN

...early December

HEADING BACK INTO THE LOCKER ROOM, I SIT ON THE bench in front of my stall and begin to remove all my gear. We just beat the Vikings 5-1 and we've maintained our recent winning streak. We keep this up and that Cup will definitely be ours come June and my sister will love me even more.

"Great game," JJ says, clapping me on the shoulder before I remove my jersey. "You were on fire out there tonight."

"You were too," I reply. "That assist with Anton will definitely make play of the day on *SportsCenter*. It was textbook perfect."

"Thanks, man," he says, shuffling over to his stall to change.

After showering, I'm in front of my stall, changing

into my suit when my phone begins to ring. I consider letting it go to voicemail but there's only one person who would be calling right now so I stand up, reach into my bag, and grab my phone but miss it as soon as my hand lands on it. It immediately begins to ring again. "Someone's impatient," I mumble as I pull it out. Sure enough, my sister's name shows on the screen. I bet the first thing she does is berate me for letting that goal in during the last seconds of the first quarter.

"Hey hey, Sissy, I know, I know what you're going to say, 'how could I let that goal slip through?'" I wait for her reply, but I'm met with silence and an uneasy feeling washes over me. "Kendall..."

Finally she speaks and that uneasy feeling intensifies when she tearfully cries my name, "Kal." She pauses and swallows back a sob. "It's...it's..." She's so distraught she can't talk right now and it's scaring me.

"What's wrong?" I shout, my voice garnering the attention of everyone in the room.

"It's Nanna and Pops," Kendall blubbers.

"What? Are they okay?" Dropping onto the bench, I rest my elbows on my knees and stare at the floor.

"They were out walking and...and they—"

"They what?" I interrupt, my voice harsher than I intended but I have a bad feeling right now.

"They didn't make it," she whispers down the line. My heart breaks at her words. "They're...they're gone, Kal."

"How? What? How?" I ask her, my heart breaking. Tears well in my eyes over the loss of the only parental figures I ever had.

"A car hit them while they were out walking. It hit...it hit black ice and...and they didn't make it." She begins to really cry now.

"Fuuuuck, I'll umm." Rubbing my hand over my face, I let out a sigh. "Let me arrange a flight and I'll be home as soon as I can."

"I need you, Kal," she pleads, "please hurry." I hate that I'm nearly five thousand kilometers away right now. I need to be there for my sister, I know Rani, her best friend will be there for her, but I'm her brother, her family. I need to be there for her.

Right now, I feel like shit for being so far away, but it's been my dream since I first held a stick in my hand to play hockey professionally. And luckily for me, I was a natural. Pops encouraged me to pursue it. He was at every game, every tournament, and he'd drive me to any hockey camp I was invited to. He was the only person I wanted with me when they announced my draft. And now, now he and Nanna are gone.

"I'm coming, Sis. I'll be in touch once I know when I'll arrive."

Hanging up from Kendall, I drop my phone to the bench next to me and let out the breath I didn't realize I was holding. Lowering my head, I close my eyes. I try and hold back the grief but the first tear falls and that opens the floodgates. The tears are now pouring down my cheeks, not manly, I know but my grandparents are, were, Kendall and my everything. Our parents don't give two shits about us. She and I are the awesome people we are today because of them. Memories of my time with them play before my closed eyes.

"Kal." A sweet angelic voice pierces through my grief and snaps my attention back to the present. "Are you okay?"

Lifting my head, I look up into the concerned eyes of the one woman who has the power to ease my pain. "Yes, no, I don't know." She sits down beside me, I don't know how she's here right now, guessing JJ summoned her but however it happened, I'm glad she's here. She takes my hand in hers and squeezes it in that reassuring way, that right now eases the pain a little. Her touch is instantly comforting and just what I need. "Nanna and Pops are gone."

"Ohh, Kal," she cries. "I'm so sorry. I know how much they meant to you."

She leans over and wraps her arms around me. That action causes the floodgates to open farther and in the middle of the locker room, I break down over the loss of my grandparents.

Vaguely I hear her talking with someone, but I can't focus on anything right now, that is until I hear Doucheman's voice. "Aww, did our precious goalie stub his toe?"

"He just lost his grandparents, jackass," Chelsea defends, in my honor.

"Everyone dies," he snarls in response.

"That's enough, Däuchmen," Coach berates him.

"I was just joking," he quickly refutes, but we all know he's full of shit. "I'm sorry for your loss," he tacks on, and you can tell from the monotone of his voice that it was insincere.

"Show some respect, boy, your parents raised you better than that." Coach squeezes my shoulder and I look up at him. "I'm sorry for your loss, Jones. Take all the time you need, family comes first."

"Thanks, sir." Nodding at him, I'm at a loss for what else to say or do. He too seems uncomfortable, without saying anything further, he walks away from me. I look to Chels sitting next to me. "I need to get home to my sister, she's a mess."

"Come on," Chels says, offering me her hand. "Let's get you home to Kendall."

The next few hours are a blur and without Chels I'd still be sitting on that bench in the locker room. We are currently sitting in first class, awaiting the trip back to Vancouver. Looking over at her, I sadly smile. "Thanks for coming with me."

"There's nowhere else I'd rather be." She reaches over and takes my hand in hers, she squeezes it and smiles. For the first time since that fateful call, I feel at ease and content. Chels has been by my side since I found out, her presence has kept me going. Staring at her as the plane hurtles down the runway, I realize that I'm hopelessly in love with this woman.

Looking over at her, I decide to tell her exactly how I feel. Losing Nanna and Pops has shown me that life can be taken away in an instant and I don't want her to not know how I feel. Hell, she gave me a chance and I will not let her down. "Chels." She turns her head and looks over at me. "I love you."

Her eyes widen and then she smiles her beautiful megawatt smile at me. She reaches up and cups my cheek in her hand. "I love you too." She leans toward me and presses her lips to mine, reaffirming her love for me.

Pulling back, I rest my forehead against hers. "I love you so much, Chelsea Maxwell. I'm never letting you go."

"I like the sound of that."

She rests her head on my shoulder as the plane finally lifts off, whisking us off to Canada for what's not going to be a fun trip home.

32

CHELSEA

Today was an emotional day and one that I don't want to feel again anytime soon. Kal and Kendall have finalized all the arrangements for the funeral, which will be held in three days' time. Their parents were a no-show at the funeral home but from what I know about them, I'm not surprised that they didn't show up.

We are back at Kendall's place, her friend Rani just left and now it's just the three of us. Rani is a hoot and has no filter. I can see why her and Kendall are besties, hell, I want to be her bestie—don't tell Margot. She has a habit of rhyming when she speaks and I think her presence really helped today, lightening the mood when it got too emotional and heavy.

Leaning into the fridge, I grab a bottle of white and fill the glasses that Kendall places on the countertop. Pouring the wine, a thought hits me as I pick up the drinks to hand them out. "Question, why is there no white wine emoji?" I ask, passing Kal and Kendall their glasses of white. "I mean, there's a red one and a bubbly one and cocktail one and a whiskey one, but no white one?" I take a sip of my wine and then continue on my white wine emoji rant. "What do the emoji peeps have against white wine?" I look at them both and wait for an answer.

"Wow, you've really thought about this, haven't you?" he says.

"Yes, yes I have."

"So you had a productive day then?" he teases me.

Sticking my tongue out at him, I shoot back, "Very productive, thank you very much, AND I had time to ponder on this very important question."

"Kal, I agree with her," Kendall adds. "It is a very important question and one I have no answer for but it's pretty discriminatory to the white wine lovers of the world."

"Yes, so very important," Kal replies with an eyeroll. "I'll be sure to contact the Pentagon and get the top brass right on it."

"Just write to Zuckerberg and ask him," Kendall nonchalantly says, taking another sip of wine. "He's more likely to create one than the Pentagon."

"Sure, I'll get right on that, Sis, since Zuck and I are BFFs," he replies with a teasing tone. I've noticed over the last few days that he and Kendall like to razz each other any chance they get.

"Don't be an ass," I scold him.

"Yeah, Kallen, don't be an ass," Kendall agrees with me. Jumping up from her seat, she slaps the island countertop. "And on that ass note, I'm taking my wine," she tops her glass up, "and going for a bath."

Kendall walks out of the kitchen, leaving Kal and me alone. He stalks over to me and wraps his arms around me. "I love your ass, does that count for the no white wine emoji?"

"No, but thank you for the ass compliment."

He reaches down and palms my ass, pulling me closer to him. "You sure you—"

"Don't even finish that sentence, Kallen Jones."

"But—"

"Nope, no butts—pun totally intended. What have I told you about my ass?" Looking up at him, I give him the 'you know what I'm talking about' look.

He deadpans, "It's a one-way passage, so back away from my ass."

He removes his hand from my ass, turns, and leans against the countertop next to me. He looks over at me and the look he's giving me right now has my body—but not my ass—zinging with desire, want, need, and everything in between.

"But..."

"Nope, no buts." I pause and tap my finger against my wine glass. "Not unless you let me shove Buzz up yours."

"Nope, it's a one-way passage."

I throw him a 'told you so' look. Then I jump up onto the countertop, lean back, and open my thighs. "My va-jay-jay however, is happy to have your cock, if you're interested."

And interested he is.

He scoops me up into his arms and stalks down to the guest room. All thoughts of my ass and there being no white wine emoji are gone. Now, all thoughts are on his cock and my va-jay-jay coming together.

If I thought the other day was tough, today was that day all over again and more. Today, we say our final goodbye to Nanna and Pops. I didn't know them like Kal and Kendall and even I'm an emotional mess. I can only imagine how they must be feeling right now.

Both Kal and Kendall are quiet and moving slowly. We'll be leaving for the service soon but no one is rushing. A knock at the door breaks the silence. "I'll get it," I tell them, but I notice that neither of them made a move. They are sitting on the sofa, Kal and Kendall have their hands linked. Both looking devastated, I don't know what to do to help them. I hate being so helpless.

The knock comes again. "Coming," I yell out. A small smile appears on Kal's face at what I just yelled out and I find myself smiling for the first time today.

Opening the door, my eyes widen when I see Mom and Dad standing there. "Mom. Dad. What are you guys doing here?" I ask them, shock evident in my voice.

"We came to pay our respects," Dad informs me like I should know why they're in front of me right now.

"In Canada?"

"That is where Kallen is from," Dad states matter-of-factly. "You going to let us in, Pumpkin?"

"Ohh, yeah, sure." Stepping aside, Mom and Dad enter Kendall's apartment. Each of them hugging me on their way past.

"Coach," Kal says, hopping up from the sofa and walking over to us. "What are you doing here?"

"Came to lend our support and offer our condolences in person." Dad and Kal shake hands. "How you holding up, son?"

"Getting there," he replies with a shrug.

"I'm so sorry, Kal," Mom murmurs, enveloping him in a mom hug. He lifts his arms and hugs her back.

Kendall joins us. "Hi, Mr. and Mrs. Maxwell, thank you for coming."

"Please, it's David and Vanessa. I'm so sorry for your loss," Mom offers. Reaching out, she squeezes Kendall's hand and Kendall starts to cry again. I'm about to pull her into my side when Mom goes into Supermom mode. "Ohh, come here," she coos and opens her arms. Kendall doesn't hesitate and she steps into Mom's open arms. She wraps her arms around Mom's waist and breaks apart, the grief overwhelming her. She cries like she did when Kal and I first arrived.

Mom is whispering to Kendall, and whatever she's saying calms her down. She pulls back and wipes the tears from her face. "Thank you." She looks to Dad and smiles but it doesn't reach her eyes, it's laced with sadness. "Kal and I appreciate you coming all this way. Can I offer you a drink?"

"That would be lovely but Chels can get it. You go and freshen up," Mom tells her.

Kendall nods and turns on her heel. We all watch her walk away. "Will she be okay?" Dad asks but before anyone can answer, Mom does.

"She will, she's a Jones and they breed 'em tough up here in Canada, eh?" Mom looks to Kal as she says this.

"That's correct, Nessa." Kal looks to me. "Want a hand making those coffees?"

"Sure." Looking to Mom and Dad, I suggest, "Take a seat and we'll be right back."

Kal and I walk into the kitchen and start making the coffees. While we wait for the pot to brew, Kal pulls me into his arms. "Did you know they were coming?"

Shaking my head, I look up at him. "Nope, I should have known that Mom would want to be here for you."

"Why me?" He scrunches his face in confusion.

"Because you mean something to me, therefore you mean something to her and when someone she loves hurts, she hurts too."

"I...I don't know what to say."

"Don't say anything, just take her hugs and allow her to cook up a storm."

"Cook?"

"Food makes everything better, duh."

He laughs and holds me tighter. "How did I get so lucky?"

"I ask myself that question each and every day."

He kisses my head and sighs. "Let's get these coffees going before Kendall gets grouchy."

"I heard that," she says from the living room.

"Truth hurts, Sis," Kal shouts back. He places one last kiss on my head and then we get to making the coffees before we head to the funeral.

33
KALLEN

Today was tough, much tougher than I envisioned but having Chels by my side made it that much more bearable. Mum and Dad, were well, Mum and Dad. Mum played the grieving daughter but as soon as they could, they left without so much as a goodbye to my sister and me. Leaving Kendall and me alone, once again.

Thankfully, Nessa was here. She looked after Kendall in a way I never could. She looked after her in that caring motherly way. In the way that *our* mother should have, but our mother is too self-involved to care about anyone but herself.

I'm still in shock that Coach and Nessa flew up for this. The team sent their condolences. JJ apologized that he couldn't be here in person. He wanted to be here to pay his respects since he and Nanna were close, but it's his sister's twenty-first birthday. Nanna wouldn't have wanted him to miss his sister's milestone birthday and I too understood. I told him drinks were on him next time we went out. That seemed to appease him, but I know JJ feels bad missing the funeral because he has a heart of gold.

"You okay?" Chelsea asks, joining me on the front porch swing. The last of the guests have left and it's just Kendall and Chelsea's parents here now.

"Yes. No. I don't know," I honestly tell her, pulling her into my side because it's friggin' cold out here, but I needed some fresh air.

"I'm here for anything you need, you just have to ask."

"Anything, hey?" I raise my eyebrows at her and this causes her to laugh.

"Play your cards right and maybe." We stare at one another intently. I bite my lip, the temperature around us rises rapidly. "Sooooo, you've always wanted to get it on with your girlfriend in your childhood bedroom?"

"This isn't the house that Kendall and I grew up in with Nanna and Pops. They downsized a few years ago when the maintenance on the big house got too much for them and FYI, I've never done that, here or there."

"You mean to tell me that Kallen Jones, sexy puck-head, never brought a girl back to his house?"

I nod at her. "Yep. I never dated anyone to bring them home."

"I find it hard to believe that Mr. Hockey never hooked up."

"Now, I never said I didn't hook up. I just never brought anyone home."

"I find that hard to believe, but what would Nanna and Pop say about you wanting to, you know, with me in their house?"

"They'd be stoked because they love...loved, you as much as I do."

"And I loved them too, but we are NOT getting it on in their house."

"We can get it on once we get back to Kendall's."

"Deal."

She rests her head on my shoulder and snuggles into my side. Wrapping my arm tighter around her, I close my eyes and breathe her in. For the first time all day, I feel at peace with the world and it's all because of the angel in my arms.

"I'm going to miss you," Kendall cries, hugging me tightly as we stand on the sidewalk at the airport.

"You can always fly back with me." I again try to convince her to come back with Chels and me.

She shakes her head. "I'll be there soon for Christmas. Besides, I need to get Nanna and Pops house listed." In their wills, Nanna and Pops left everything they had to Kendall and me. Mum wasn't impressed to be left out of her parents' will, but what did she expect?

After a lengthy discussion, Kendall and I decided to

sell the house because a family home isn't what either of us wants right now.

"I don't think you should do that alone," she goes to interrupt, but I place my finger over her lips, "but I know that you want and need to do this, so I'll allow it."

"You'll allow it, really? You're not the boss of me and as the oldest, I'm the boss of you."

"Damn women, ganging up on me," I whine.

"You love it, Kal. Now, I need to go before that security guard over there goes all Hulk on me." She turns to Chelsea. "It was great to see you again and I'll be in touch before I fly over for Christmas."

"You better." Chels wraps her arms around her. She whispers something that I can't hear but it must be sweet because Kendall smiles and then laughs.

"Oh. My. God," she screeches, "you are friggin perfect for my brother. I'm so glad you decided to give him a chance."

"Yeah, me too," she says, looking at me and smiling.

Pulling my sister in for one last hug, I hold on tighter and longer than usual. "I love you, Sis."

"I love you too, Baby Bro, and remember, don't fuck my team up."

A laugh escapes me. "You do realize it's a team sport."

"I know that but I'm holding you personally responsible for any losses."

"No pressure, now you better go, Hulk is about to Hulk out."

We have one last hug before Kendall jumps back into her Jeep and pulls away from the curb. Chels and I watch her drive off and out of sight before we head into the terminal to check-in.

After what feels like a million hours, we finally make it back to my apartment. "I'm exhausted," I whine before collapsing onto my bed.

"You and me both," Chels agrees. "I'm too tired to go home."

"Even if you weren't, I want you to stay."

"I'm not having sex with you."

"Good, I'm too tired for that. I just want to go to sleep with you in my arms."

"That I can manage."

She begins to strip off her clothes and my cock, even though I'm dead tired, likes the view of her in only her panties. Rearranging myself, Chels shakes her head. "Really? Me changing turns you on?" she teases as she slips one of my Crusher shirts over her head and walks into the en suite to brush her teeth.

"Not my fault that my girlfriend is sexy as puck." Climbing off the bed, I strip down to my briefs and join her in the en suite. Standing next to her, I squeeze some paste onto my brush and begin to brush mine. I notice her eyes raking over my body.

"Like what you see?" I mumble around my brush.

She nods in agreement. "Immensely." She spits and rinses her brush. With our eyes locked on one another in the mirror, I brush my teeth and she begins to brush her hair. She places her brush down on the vanity and then the minx trails her fingertip across my shoulders, down my back, and squeezes my ass before walking back into the bedroom.

I finish brushing my teeth and when I walk back into the bedroom, Chelsea is lying on her back under the covers with her eyes closed. Her hair is splayed out underneath her like a golden halo. Picking up my phone, I snap a photo, she looks so peaceful and beautiful.

"You right there creeping on me while I sleep?" she mumbles with her eyes closed.

"How did you know I was staring?"

"I can always feel when you're around. Now, are you coming to bed? Or are you going to stand there like a creeper?"

"I think you know the answer to that."

"Fine, creep away but do it quietly, I need my beauty sleep."

"You don't need sleep to be beautiful."

"Thank you for the compliment, but shhhh, I'm trying to sleep."

"You're bossy when you're sleepy."

"Shhhh, sleeping," she growls with a smile on her beautiful face.

Climbing under the covers, I pull her into me so we are spooning. "Night, Chels."

"Night, Kal." She kisses my hand and snuggles into me, wriggling her butt on my cock.

"You keep that up and I'm going to have to fuck you."

"Mmmhmpf," she whispers while continuing to grind her ass on me.

"I thought you were tired."

"I am but I think I might need a little nightcap to help me drift off."

"I think I can help you with that." Sliding my hand

down, I reach up under the hem of my shirt and I find her bare. "What happened to your panties."

"I took them off."

"I like your style, Chelsea Maxwell." She lifts her leg over me, opening herself up. My fingers slide between her folds, she's already wet for me so my fingers easily slip inside.

"And I like your style, Kallen Jones," she purrs as I begin to slide my fingers in and out of her.

Freeing my cock with my other hand, I slide it between her cheeks, her body tenses, until she feels the tip at her entrance. Removing my fingers from her, I press down on her clit, earning a pleasurable moan. She wriggles her hips and my cock slides inside. Turning her head toward me, she kisses me deeply. Our tongues slipping and sliding in and out of each other's mouths while our hips rock back and forth. Moving my hand up her body, I cup her breast in my palm, tweaking her nipple between my thumb and forefinger. Languidly, we rock back and forth, making love to one another.

It's slow.

It's sensual.

It's perfect in every way.

Her breathing picks up and she pulls her lips from mine. Melding her body into mine, I feel her body begin to tense. "Come for me, baby," I whisper into her ear, biting her earlobe. Nibbling her neck, she moans my name as her orgasm takes over. Her pussy clenches down on my cock and it sets me off, together we come and ride out the euphoria enveloping us.

We lie wrapped in each other's arms, breathing heavily.

"Night, Kal," she sleepily murmurs.

"Night, Chels," I reply. "I love you." But she's already asleep. Closing my eyes, I drift off to sleep happy and content.

34

CHELSEA

...early February

TIME IS FLYING BY. IT FEELS LIKE JUST YESTERDAY IT was Christmas but next week is Valentine's Day and for the first time in a long time, I'm excited for the commercial holiday. *He* wasn't very romantic so I'm excited to see what Kal has in store for me.

He's been sheepish and aloof the last few weeks with me, so I presume it has something to do with a surprise for me next week. But then the stupid voice in my head is wondering if he's cheating on me. I need to stop letting the taunts that *he* keeps spouting in. Kal isn't *him* and he wouldn't cheat on me or use me, he's not a douche.

"Pumpkin," Dad says from the doorway to my office —it's so weird having my own office here.

"What's up, Daddy-o?" When I look up from my

computer, I see a look on his face that has me immediately on alert. "What's wrong?"

"I, well, Jackie in marketing wants you to do something."

"And?"

He squeezes the back of his neck. "They want you to do a team profile."

"Sure, no worries, I had plans to do that in the lead up to the playoffs."

"They want individual profiles."

"Yeah, sure, I can do that."

"They want individual videos and segments."

"Okay, I don't see an issue there. Is there anything else specific that they want?"

"You have to include Däuchmen...one-on-one."

"Ohh, I didn't think of that."

"That's why Jackie in marketing asked me to talk to you. They're worried about you and him."

Leaning back in my chair, I tap my finger on my chin and then smile. "They have nothing to worry about because A. I'm a professional, and B. I have a plan and it's a tweak on what they want BUT it will be better. Let me put it down on paper and then I'll run it by Jackie, make it seem like my idea is better than hers, which it is, and then I won't need any one-on-one time with *him*."

Daddy smiles and shakes his head side to side. "You continue to amaze me, Pumpkin. I've been shitting bricks having to tell you this."

"Dad," I deadpan, "I'm a professional but thankfully for me, I'm also smart and can work my way around having to deal with *him*." Then I laugh, "Ohh, and I'm gonna need the coaching staff involved too."

"Why?"

"Because it's all part of the 'don't spend one-on-one time with Däuchmen' plan."

"Man, I wish I could just fire his ass."

"I know, me too, but we have to work with what we've got, and unfortunately, that includes *him* AND it now means, YOU get to be involved in this."

"Pucking Däuchmen and you, miss, are lucky that I love you."

"Everyone loves me," I nonchalantly tell him. "Now, shoo, I have a non-one-on-one team marketing plan to iron out."

Dad shakes his head and exits my office, mumbling to himself about women being bossy.

Opening a new file, I begin to jot down what I have in mind for the campaign. I feel like someone is watching me and when I lift my gaze from the computer screen, I internally groan when I see *him* leaning against the door-frame to my office. "Can I help you, Stefan?" My voice gives away how much I don't want to be talking to him.

"You know he's just using you."

And we're back on this bandwagon, I think to myself. Lowering the lid on my MacBook, I cross my arms and lean my elbows on my desk. "Ohh, really, and how is he using me?"

His eyes drop to my chest, he licks his lips and I shudder. How I ever used to love this man is mind boggling. "My eyes are up here, Stefan."

"You still have a nice rack," he lewdly replies. "I remember how much you used to love me suckling and playing with them."

Ignoring that statement, I focus on why he's here. "You were going to explain to me how Kal is using me?"

"Ohh yes, your precious, Kal."

"I'm waiting."

"He's using you to get ahead in the game. Daddy dearest has taken him under his wing, something that Coach has never ever done before. He's also dropping the Maxwell name all over the place, how do you think he landed the Nike deal? Dropped Coach Maxwell's name and boom, million-dollar deal."

"Like Dad has any sway with Nike."

"You'd be surprised."

"You're just jealous that I've moved on."

"No, concerned for you," he retorts and for a brief moment, I believe the sincerity in his voice...and then I remember what he did to me.

"Where was your concern for me when you were screwing those puck bunnies in our bed?"

"Believe me. Don't believe me. Just don't come running to me crying when his deceit and lies come to light, but feel free to come running to me for a decent fuck."

Before I can tell him to piss off, he leaves.

Staring at the empty doorway, I shake off the encounter with *him* and get back to work. I focus on this new marketing thing, but no matter how hard I try, *his* words keep playing over and over in my head. Do I have my blinders on when it comes to Kal? Or is he just jealous that I've moved on?

Little did I know, this marketing plan, even with its tweak was going to implode in a way that I never imagined.

35

KALLEN

Tomorrow is Valentine's Day and I cannot wait to spend the day with Chelsea. I have it all planned out. This sneaking around the last few weeks has been hard. Thankfully, I was finalizing the Gatorade deal, thanks to Jaxson—yep, I signed on with him and Life's Too Sport—so I used that as an excuse to disappear when needed. I just need to get this thing today over and done with, so I can nut out the final pieces and pick up part of my present for Chelsea.

A few weeks back we were wandering around SoHo and we went into this little gallery. There was a painting that Chels fell in love with, she's been raving about it for weeks now. When I went into the gallery to purchase it, the artist just so happened to be there. He and I got to chatting and I was telling him all about Chels and the love she has for the piece. He grabbed a Sharpie off the counter and signed the back of the canvas with a personal message for Chels. He didn't have to do that but I'm so glad he did because it makes this gift that much more personal and perfect now.

I'm snapped back to the present when Doucheman shoulder-barges me, his usual greeting. One of these days, I'm going to snap and my fist is going to become acquainted with his face...repeatedly.

"You guys all set?" an angelic voice says from the doorway to the family lounge. Looking up, I see my sexy as hell girlfriend standing there in a purple Crushers' tank tucked into jeans that should be illegal.

We all nod our heads and murmur yes.

"Great, first up I'll have Anton." He jumps up and walks toward Chels. "You're on your own since you're the team captain, hope that's okay?"

"All good, Chels."

"Sweet. Head on down to the rink and I'll be there in five." She looks back to the rest of us. "Kal and JJ, you'll be next and then Stefan, Jett, and Cliff, you three will finish up the day today. Then tomorrow morning will be everyone else and then we'll finish the day with the group thing. Then I just have to work my magic and voila, all done."

"Why is marketing crap always fun with you?" Jett asks her, "but when marketing marketing arranges it, it's like watching paint dry."

Everyone nods in agreement because it's true, marketing people are the most boring people out there. You'd think with their creativity it would be fun all the time.

"'Cause I'm awesome," she says, a smile gracing her

face. Since taking on this social media roll, Chels has really flourished. Watching her come into herself has been great to see. No longer is she just known as the coach's daughter, she's known as our kickass social media lady. She was always carefree and fun, but now it's tenfold.

"Yeah, you are," I tell her, blowing her a kiss across the room. She pretends to catch up and tucks it into her jeans pocket. JJ groans and rolls his eyes and so he isn't left out, I do the same to him. The dick that he is, mimics Chelsea's reaction and I can't help but laugh.

"All right you two," Chelsea chastises us. "When Anton comes back, you two come on down."

"*The Price is Right*," JJ singsongs. We all shake our head at his dramatics. You can always count on him for a laugh, even if just now Chels did look like a game show hostess with the hand gestures.

"Just don't make me wait, guys, I want this done and dusted before four, I have something I need to do." Her eyes are locked on me and from the smoldering look she's giving me, I have a feeling I know what she needs to do... we discussed it last week and she told me that for Valentine's Day she'd do it.

Walking over to her, I place a quick kiss on her lips before she heads out to the ice to oversee her project.

"And now they're giving each other fuck-me eyes," JJ groans as I turn around to face him, shaking my head. Thankfully, Chelsea is already gone so she didn't hear him.

"You're just jealous that my girlfriend is hotter than your girlfri...ohh that's right, you don't have one."

"I'm trying," he snaps and I notice his gaze drifts off and I bet he's thinking about Lexi. Like seriously, those two just need to fuck and get on with things.

I'm about to tell him to make his grand gesture toward her when Doucheman stops in front of me. "Däuchmen," I tersely say.

"She's going to wake up and smell the fakeness one of these days and then she's going to dump your sorry ass and come crawling back to me."

"One, I'm not fake. Two, she will never go back to you, and three, I don't give a flying fuck what you think." The tone of my voice garners the attention of Coach, who's conferring with the trainers. He gives me a 'you need to calm down' kind of look. I know he's right, but I cannot stand this asshole and I'm close to snapping.

"You think I don't know what you're up to?"

"Enlighten me then Douche-man." I place emphasis on the word douche.

"You hook up with the coach's daughter just as the season starts, playing dumb like you didn't know who she was. Then all of a sudden, you guys are dating and then Coach becomes your BFF and suddenly, you're getting all these endorsement deals because no doubt you keep throwing the Maxwell name around." His gaze lands on something behind me but he's really just pissed me off. Stepping into his personal space, I stare into his smarmy face, clenching my teeth. From the corner of my eye, I can see Coach walking toward me but there's no need, I'm fine.

"Yes, you got me, Stefan, my secret is out. I'm fucking Chels so I can get an in with her dad and land myself all these endorsement deals. Now that I have Gatorade locked in and about to sign on the dotted line on another one, I don't need her. I can finally hook up with the bunnies when we travel to Toronto next week because I've gotten what I need. I don't need Chelsea anymore 'cause I got what I want. You—"

Someone from behind me gasps and when I turn around, I'm met with the tear-stained and hurt face of Chels.

"Told you he was using you," Däuchmen snarls from behind me. He slaps my shoulder and smirks a sinister smirk at me. "Enjoy dealing with the psycho that is Chelsea Maxwell when she loses good dick...not that I'm sure it was good with you."

He walks over to Chels, placing his finger under her chin and lifts her tear-filled gaze to his. "You know where to find me after you lay into him." Leaning down he presses his lips to hers.

That's the final straw. I see red. Walking over, I pull him away from her. Spinning him around, I slam my fist into his face. Repeatedly I hit him until someone pulls me off him. I'm fuming that he trapped and goaded me like he did.

"Enough, Kallen," someone shouts and that's when I look down and notice Stefan's face is bloody and swollen. Pulling myself free, I turn around and see a concerned and angry Coach glaring at me. And hidden behind him, a broken and defeated Chels.

Putting one foot in front of the other, I walk over to her. "Chels," I quietly say, but she shakes her head and raises her hand in a stop motion. She turns and runs away from me.

Däuchmen laughs like the maniac he is and I crumple to my knees, not knowing what exactly she heard, but regardless of what she heard, it's all been misconstrued because Doucheman walked me into a trap, and I have a horrible feeling that I just lost the best thing to ever happen to me.

36
CHELSEA

"My secret is out. I'm fucking Chels so I can get an in with her dad and land myself all these endorsement deals. Now that I have Gatorade locked in and about to sign on the dotted line on another one, I don't need her. I can finally hook up with the bunnies when we travel to Toronto next week because I've gotten what I need. I don't need Chelsea anymore 'cause I got what I want."

Hearing Kal confirm all the things that *he* has been warning me about was a sucker punch to the gut, but seeing him attack Stefan like he did, that was truly terrifying. I don't know Kal like I thought I did and what's worse, Stefan was right.

Racing out of the room, I head up to my office, I need to get out of here and away from Kal and this mess. Bending down, I grab my handbag from the bottom drawer and when I stand up, Kal is standing in the doorway.

"Chels—"

Lifting my hand in a stop motion, I shake my head. "No, Kal, I...no."

"What he's saying is horseshit."

"Is it? He's been warning me for months now that you aren't who you're pretending to be, and just now, what I heard confirms everything he said. And...and the way you beat him, that's not the Kallen Jones I know." Shaking my head, my eyes begin to well with tears again. "I don't know you," I whisper, the first tear drops and cascades down my cheek. "I don't know you."

"You do know me, Chels. No one knows me like you do." He walks into my office and comes around my desk. I move around the other way. He's now behind my desk and I'm in the doorway. The hurt on his face at the separation between us is confusing. "Please, Chels, you know me."

"Do I?" I angrily throw back at him. "You just confirmed ev-rey-thing he's warned me about. I thought he was just being a douche of an ex but now, now I don't know what to believe. I'm so confused right now."

"Ask me anything and I'll answer it honestly."

"Did you drop dad's name to get the *Gatorade* deal?"

"Not in the way you think. I told them that David Maxwell has taken me under his wing and he's a great mentor, that's it."

"Did you use me to make your rookie year phenomenal?"

"I can't believe you're asking me that," he growls.

"Answer the question, Kal. Did. You. Use. Me?" I pause between each of the last four words for emphasis.

"I can't believe you're asking me that," he repeats again, and his non-answer is answer enough.

"I'm done, Kal. Done." Turning on my heel, I exit my office. My heart breaks with each step I take toward the stairs. As if fate is rubbing all this in my face, "Someone You Love" by Lewis Capaldi is playing and he's singing about the rug being pulled out from under you, perfect analogy for my life right now.

Someone grabs my arm and I know it's Kal because even with my heart breaking, the air around us still sizzles. Pulling my arm free, I turn to face him.

"Please, Chels," he begs, taking my hands in his, squeezing tightly.

Shaking my head, I pull my hand free and stare at the man I love. Loved? I stare at the man who just broke my heart to smithereens. "You...you promised not to puck me around and from everything that's right in front of me, you did. I pucking hate you, Kallen Jones, and I never want to see you again."

Turning on my heel, I walk away from him. Before I push the door open, I stop and look over my shoulder. "I pucking hate that I love you," I tearfully whisper.

Putting one foot in front of the other, I walk away from him. I run through the players' entrance and out into the rain. Of course it's raining because my day wasn't shitty enough already. He was just like *him,* a pucking puckhead. Once again, I have a broken heart because of a puckhead. I should have stuck to my rules, but no, my stupid heart had to go and fall for someone I swore I never would. He's a liar, a big fat pucking using liar.

I'm done with men.

Done with love.

I pucking hate him but I also still pucking love him...
I'm so pucking screwed.

37

CHELSEA

With my head down, I run through the parking garage, the need to get away from the arena and hide out in my apartment is overwhelming me. My heart is shattering right now at the betrayal—and what's worse—*he* was right. I was being used and now I'm the sucker that's been pucked over...twice.

The rain is pelting down and before I even make it to the corner, I'm soaked through. Waiting for the crosswalk to change to green, my phone rings, again, and like the last however many times since I ran out, I ignore it. Finally, the light changes to green and I step out to cross the road. Someone shouts out my name and from the tone of their voice, something isn't right. I look up and freeze when I see a bus sliding sideways toward me. The road is slick and wet, the bus is out of control and careening toward me. A normal person would move out of the way but I'm frozen on the spot. My feet are glued to the road, the bus getting closer and closer and then suddenly, I'm flying through the air before landing on the asphalt with a thud.

My head cracks on the ground and the wind is knocked out of me. Breathing is hard and my vision begins to dot. A figure stands above me, their words are muffled and everything is blurry. My body is fuzzy and my eyelids feel like they have lead weights attached to them. I can't keep blinking so I close my eyes and let the darkness engulf me.

When I come too, there's a light above me, I'm strapped down and there's something around my neck and I'm wet. Blinking rapidly to clear my vision, I realize I'm in an ambulance. What? Why? How? Then it all comes back to me.

Hearing Kal confirm he's using me.

Kal trying to deny it.

Running out of the arena.

It's raining.

A bus coming at me.

Flying through the air

...and then nothing.

"You're awake," a cheerful voice says from beside me. Turning my eyes, I see a petite brunette in a paramedic uniform. "How you feeling?"

"Like I was hit by a bus," I honestly tell her, my body pucking hurts right now.

"You almost were," she confirms.

"Huh?" I question, completely confused right now. I remember a bus but nothing after that.

"A bus's brakes failed and from what I was told, it

was careening toward you and then one of the hockey players from nearby knocked you out of harm's way."

"Was anyone hurt?"

"Just you and the man who saved you." She pauses.

"That's good but what man? And is he okay?"

"I don't know his name but he's on his way to the hospital too. Eyewitnesses say he came out of nowhere and prevented you from getting hit by the bus. He was still being assessed when we loaded you in, but from what I overheard, he was unconscious but no other physical injuries. You're both very lucky."

Closing my eyes, my body rocks side to side as the ambulance takes me toward the hospital and I wonder which of the players was my rescuer.

We arrive at the hospital and I'm whisked into a cubicle. The paramedic is reading out stats and saying things that I have no clue about. Then a nurse is attaching a blood pressure cuff and placing that little thingy on my finger to count my pulse and oxygen levels. FYI, it's called a pulse oximeter but I prefer little thingy on my finger.

I'm sent for a CT scan of my head, an X-ray on my wrist, and they draw blood, not sure why they need blood, but who am I to question the medical peeps.

Both the CT and my X-ray come back clear. I have a sprained wrist, which they bandage up, and thankfully it's my left one and not my right one. My only other injury, a bruise forming along my jawline, probably from when I hit the ground.

The doctor has just left to follow up on my blood tests. If he's happy with them, then he'll arrange my discharge papers since I don't have any significant injuries. Thankfully, I don't have a concussion, just a nasty bump to the head.

The curtain opens again. "That was quick," I say but when I look up, Mom and Dad are standing there. "Mom. Dad, what are you doing here?"

"Well, when your daughter is in the hospital, her parents generally want to attend and make sure she's okay," Dad states. Walking over to me he places a kiss on my temple and looks down at me. "You okay, Pumpkin?"

Nodding, I wince as my head is still a little tender. "I'm fine, is..." I drift off as I don't know who saved me. "Is whoever saved me okay?"

"He's still being assessed at the moment," Mom informs me, taking a seat next to me. She squeezes my hand. "I'm so glad you're okay, Chels. When Daddy called to let me know you were nearly hit by a bus, my heart stopped beating. I'm so thankful that he saved you."

"Boy's a hero," Dad confirms.

I'm about to ask who my hero is when the curtain to my room is pulled back and a worried Margot appears. "Chelsea Maxwell, don't you ever do that to me again. I nearly had a heart attack when Nessa called me to say you were hit by a bus—"

"Nearly," I interrupt her, "nearly hit by a bus, but thankfully someone rescued me."

"And so he should have, extra brownie points for him but I'm sure you can make it up to him." Margot raises her eyebrows at me and winks.

Dad groans.

Mom smirks.

I scrunch my face up in confusion, I don't know who she's referring to.

"Who rescued me?" I ask the one question that's been burning on my tongue since I discovered I had a rescuer.

"Kallen," Margot states as if I should know this.

"Why would he rescue me?"

"Duh, he loves you and didn't want to see you squished by a bus." She turns her attention to Dad. "Speaking of, how is he?"

"Still waiting to hear."

Rapidly blinking, I try to process why Kal would rescue me. He doesn't care about me, so why would he care if I got hit by a bus or not? "Why would he rescue me?" I ask again.

"What do you mean why, sweetie?" Mom asks me, taking a seat on the edge of the bed.

"We...he...before, why would he rescue me when we just had a fight and broke up."

"You broke up? Why?" Margot screeches.

"Is this because of what happened with Stefan?" Dad probes me, confusion marring his face. I nod and again wince, I must remember to move slowly. "Stefan goaded him, Pumpkin. JJ told me exactly what went down, sure his reaction was unacceptable—"

"Unacceptable," I snap, "it's unacceptable that he's been using me just to get those endorsement deals and have you be his mentor and make his rookie year amazing."

"What are you talking about?" Dad questions me again.

"I heard what he said to Stefan, Dad. He confirmed everything that Stefan has been warning me about since he and I started dating."

"Like you'd believe anything that comes from that douche's mouth. Kal is the best thing to ever happen to you." Hearing my best friend defend the man who just smashed my heart to smithereens pisses me off.

"You're taking his side?" I snap at her. "You're taking the side of the man who lied and used me? Taking the side of the man that everything Stefan warned me about was confirmed today? I overheard him confirm everything."

"Chels, Pumpkin," Dad interrupts. "You misheard him. Stefan was taunting Kallen. I have no doubt he saw you coming and goaded Kallen into confirming what he said. That boy loves you to the moon and back, he's not using you, Pumpkin."

"But the Gatorade deal..."

"Is a deal he earned on his own. He asked me for my opinion and I gave it, but I assure you, I did nothing else, besides, I don't have any influence with them."

That's when it hits me, Stefan was being his usual douche self. He lied; this is all my fault. "This is all my fault," I begin to cry. "Is...is Kal going to be okay?"

"I don't know, Pumpkin."

"I need to see him." I pull at the cuff on my arm. "I need to apologize. I need to be there when he wakes up. I need him to know I love him and believe him and that I'm sorry."

"And you will, honey," Mom placates me, covering

my hand that's pulling at the cuff, "but first, you need to look after you."

"But I love him, Mom."

"I know that and he knows that too. All couples fight, if it was all sunshine and roses, life would be boring."

"But—"

"No buts, now lie back and wait for the doctor." Mom looks over to Margot. "Can you run to Chelsea's place and grab her some dry clothes?"

She nods and places a kiss on my head. "Back soon, chicky babe." Before I can reply, she's gone.

"David, go check on Kallen. Chels and I will patiently wait here for news."

Without saying a word, Dad kisses me on the head and exits my cubicle. My eyes are locked on the curtain, waiting for news on Kal, and waiting until I can go and see him. I need to grovel and hope that he'll take me back.

38

KALLEN

I*N SLOW MOTION* I *WATCH AS SHE STEPS OUT INTO* the street when the light changes to green. Then I notice the bus closer and closer to her. "Chelsea!" I yell again and increase my speed to get to her. I scream her name repeatedly, but the rain is coming down so hard she can't hear me.

Finally, she looks up but rather than moving out of the way, she freezes. "Moooooove," I bellow, but she doesn't. She's frozen in the middle of the road, watching the bus careen toward her.

Faster than I've ever run before, I make it to her just before the vehicle collides with her. I throw my body weight into her and we fall out of harm's way. With the speed I was running and the jump, we both fly through the air. We both land on the asphalt, hard. Her chin collides with my head and the wind is knocked out of me.

I quickly roll her off me and stand up, I need to make sure Chels is okay.

Standing above her, she blinks a few times and then her eyes close and stay shut. "Chels, babe, can you hear me?" I shout, but she doesn't wake up. Thankfully, she's still breathing but she's out cold.

"Someone call 9-1-1!" I bellow just as I begin to wobble on my feet. My vision starts to dot. I can't hold myself up. My knees collapse beneath me, and I fall to the pavement next to an out cold Chels.

The last thing I see before losing consciousness is Chels's lifeless body.

When I wake next, I'm in a hospital bed. There's a beeping from the machine attached to me but I don't see any other injuries. As if sensing I'm awake, a nurse enters, checks my stats, leaves, and returns with my doctor a few minutes later.

He informs me that I have no concussion and they think I passed out from an adrenaline crash after saving Chels from that out-of-control bus. Every time I close my eyes, that scene plays on a loop in my mind. Each time, when I see her step out, my heart literally stops beating, just like it did on the street. I still can't believe that I got to her in time. I ran faster than I ever have before to save her from impact and injury.

JJ informed me that Chels is okay and will be

discharged shortly. Hearing she's uninjured is such a relief. We were both lucky in the scheme of things.

While waiting for Doc Michels to come and assess me before clearing me to leave, I close my eyes and once again drift off to sleep. When I wake again, the aches and pains have set in. Can I just say, rescuing your girlfriend, ahh ex-girlfriend, from getting hit by a bus isn't as smooth as in the movies? My body hurts from head to toe and I have a new pain that wasn't there before. There's a pressure on my right hand that's oddly comforting.

The pressure squeezes and then I hear a muffled voice. "Please, Kal, you have to be okay. I'm sorry for listening to *him*. I'm sorry for the things I said. I'm sorry for everything." She swallows back another sob. "I pucking love you, Kallen Jones. Please come back to me. Please."

"I pucking love you too, Chelsea Maxwell."

She lifts her head and stares at me. She blinks rapidly and then smiles when she sees me staring back at her. She swallows back another sob and tears begin to streak down her cheeks. Lifting my hand that she's not holding, I cup her cheek in my palm and run the pad of my thumb gently along her bruised jawbone.

"I'm so sorry, Kal, this is all my fault. I...I let *him* get to me and now you're in the hospital and...and..." She's so upset, she can't finish her sentence. She stands up and throws herself across me, I wince at the pain, but I push through because she needs me right now.

Wrapping my arms around her, I quietly whisper, "Shhhh," and rub gentle calming circles on her back. "It's okay, Chels," I repeat again. "Everything is okay."

"No, it's not," she blubbers into my chest. "We almost got hit by a bus because I foolishly let *him* get into my mind. Deep down I know you wouldn't have done those things but hearing the words pass through your lips, for a moment, I believed them." She lifts her head and stares down at me. "Can you ever forgive me, Kal?"

"Of course," I agree. "On one condition."

"Anything!"

"You need to dig out that sexy nurse's outfit and use your lips to make everything all better."

"That's not anything a father needs to hear," Coach says from the doorway to my room.

"Can you suddenly get amnesia?" I throw back at him.

"Done," he replies and walks over to my bed. "How you feeling?"

"I feel like I got hit by a bus."

"Kal," Chels berates me and slaps my arm, "too soon."

"Technically, he didn't get hit by a bus but he saved you from a bus, therefore, he can say whatever the hell he wants. The man's a hero in my eyes." Coach clenches the rail at the end of my bed. "Thank you for saving my Pumpkin. I'll forever be in your debt."

"I'd do anything for her, Coach," I tell him and I mean every word. "Chelsea is my everything and I'd walk into the depths of hell to save her."

"That's all a father can ask for. Now, rest up, I need you back on the ice."

"Always thinking about the game," Chels teases her

dad, then she looks to me. "And with Nurse Chelsea looking after you, you'll be back on your feet in no time."

"Aaaaand, that's my cue to leave," Coach groans. "Glad you're okay, Jones, and thank you again for saving my daughter."

Before I can reply, he exits my room, the door clicking shut behind him. Looking over at Chels, I see nothing but love in her eyes reflecting back at me. "Sooo, you think Nurse Chelsea could help with a sponge bath?" I raise my eyebrows at her.

"I definitely think she can help with that." Much to my disappointment, it takes three days to get my sexy sponge bath, but it was totally worth the wait.

Chelsea has stayed with me night and day since I was discharged from the hospital, Kendall offered to fly down but I told her I was fine. It wasn't until Chelsea reassured my sister that I was in good hands that she relented and agreed to stay in Vancouver. I do, however, have to Face-Time her twice a day.

I've just gotten off the phone with Kendall and I can hear water running in my en suite. Throwing my phone onto the kitchen countertop, I walk into my bedroom and I come to a halt when I reach the doorway. Exiting the en suite in her sexy slutty nurse costume is my sexier than puck girlfriend.

"The nurse will see you now," she huskily purrs, running her fingertip between the valley of her breasts. Her dress is unzipped to below her breasts, her very naked breasts. All I can see is her cleavage and the outline of her nipples. With her fingertip, she draws circles over her chest and between her delectable tits.

With her eyes locked on mine, she circles her nipple. Then she slips her hand between her breasts and grabs the zipper. Gripping the tab between her fingers, ever so slowly, she tugs on it, exposing her stomach and panty-covered pussy. Once it's free, she rests her hands on her hips. Somehow, the material doesn't fall off her shoulders or open, all the bits I want to see are still covered underneath the white cotton.

She lifts her hand and beckons me forward with her index finger. Biting her lip, she watches me through her hooded gaze as I stalk toward my sexy slutty nurse, ready for my sponge bath and to take any other medicine she wants to administer.

39

CHELSEA

I'VE NEVER DONE ANYTHING SO SEXUAL LIKE THIS before, sure, I wore this when Kal had his altercation on the ice with *him*, but I just rode him dressed as the sexy nurse. This time, I've put on a show as his sexy nurse, and I think I want to take it further.

Beckoning him to me, I take the time to appreciate my sexy as puck boyfriend. My eyes trail down his body, he's only wearing sweats and from the considerable bulge I can see tenting them, he likes the show so far.

He stops in front of me. My breathing picks up as he takes the final step toward me. Pressing my lips to his, I kiss down his neck. Trailing little pecks all over his chest and abdomen before dropping to my knees. With my eyes locked on his, I reach into his sweats and lower them down. He kicks them off, leaving him gloriously naked before me. His cock standing to attention, the tip glistening with his arousal.

Reaching up, I grip the base of his shaft and begin to stroke him. Leaning forward, my tongue darts out, licking the tip. Opening wide, I suck the tip deep into my throat, gagging a little when it hits the back. Repeating the process a few times, I pull his dick from my mouth, wiping at the side.

His eyes widen at me no longer sucking him. "Patience," I whisper.

Staring up at him, I push my breasts together, squeezing my mounds through the cotton of my dress. A smirk appears on his face when he realizes what I'm about to do. Shuffling closer to him, I slide his shaft between my breasts. Pushing my breasts closer together, he thrusts his hips back and forth as I continue to push my boobs together around him.

"I'm...I'm going to come if you keep that up," he breathlessly murmurs.

"Do it," I demand, we repeat the action a few more times and then his body stiffens and shudders. The first spurt of creamy white cum hits my tits and chest. Pushing them together tighter, my breasts milk him until he's spent.

"Fuuuuck," he groans, sliding himself out from between my boobs. "That was..."

"Yep," I agree. "Now it's time for your sponge bath."

"I think it's you who needs a bath."

Lifting up from my knees, I turn away from him and walk into the en suite. When I reach the entrance, I lift my hands and pull the costume off my shoulders. It slides down my arms and flitters to the tiles below, leaving me only in my panties. Hooking my fingers into the waistband, I bend over, pushing them down my thighs, giving him an unobstructed view of my ass and pussy. Stepping out of them, I turn to face Kal. His eyes are hooded and his gaze rakes over my cum-addled chest, he licks his lips. "Do you know how fucking hot you look naked, with my cum all over your tits?"

"Tell me," I pant.

"How about I show you." Before I can reply, he stalks over to me, grips my cheeks in his palms, and covers my mouth with his. His tongue thrusts into my mouth. His cock is once again hard and poking into my belly.

I'm overcome with want. Need. Desire. I need him to fuck me or I'm going to combust. I cover his hands with mine. "Please," I beg against his lips.

He pulls back a fraction. "Please what?"

"Please, Kal."

"Please what?" he demands again.

"Fuck me, Kal. I need you to fuck me." I don't swear often, but right now I'm ready to combust. I don't want him to make love to me, I want him to fuck me hard and fast.

"As you wish," he utters. Spinning me around, he walks us over to the vanity. Pushing me forward, I rest my hands on the edge. He steps in behind me, caging me in. Lowering my head, I look to the floor, waiting for him to thrust into me. "Eyes on me, gorgeous," he growls.

Lifting my gaze to his in the mirror, he grips my hips roughly in his hands. He runs the tip of his shaft between my cheeks, my eyes widen, he knows how I feel about that. Then he pushes himself between my thighs. "You're soaked," he whispers just as the head of his dick pushes in. He pulls back and I moan at the loss and then groan in delight when he thrusts back inside.

With our eyes locked on one another, he thrusts in and out of me. Over and over, he thrusts into me. Removing my hand from the counter, I slide it between my thighs and press my clit. That little bundle of nerves comes alive at the pressure. Circling my finger, I slide my finger up and down my clit in time to Kal's cock slipping in and out of me.

He leans forward, pressing his front to my back and he really drives his cock into me. I've never felt pleasure like this before, I'm so close to crashing over the edge when Kal wraps his arm around me and pulls me into an upright position. His hand massages my breast, when he pinches my nipple, it sends me over the edge. I scream his name and the orgasm of all orgasms ripples through my body.

My inner porn star comes to the surface and I grunt and groan as the euphoria that only comes from being with Kal courses through me. I'm still coming down from my high when Kal comes. He squeezes me tight as he empties himself inside me.

He lets me go, his dick slips out of me, and I turn around to face him. "That...that was everything," I breathlessly inform him.

"You ain't seen nothing yet."

But I shake my head, not only is my vagina well and truly pucked right now, but he's also still recovering from playing superhero. What we just did got waaaay out of hand, I was only planning on blowing him but as with each time Kal and I get down and dirty, it gets reeeeally dirty. "Kal, you just got out of the hospital—"

"I'm fine," he interrupts me.

"You might think you are but I'm not risking it. Now, we can either shower together or I can run us a bath. Your choice?"

"So no more sexy nurse?"

"Not today but if you behave, maybe she can come visit again soon."

"Fine," he huffs. "Bath...and I make no promises that my hands won't go exploring."

"As long as your penis stays away from my vagina, I'll allow it."

"You've turned into nasty nurse. I prefer when you're sexy-slutty-want-to-fuck-me nurse."

"And you've turned into whiny cry baby patient."

"Have not." He storms over to the bath, leans down to put the plug in. When he stands up, he wobbles on his feet.

"See, you're not fine. Now sit." I point to the edge of the bath. "I'll get this."

"Yeah, okay."

"Did you just agree with me?" I tease.

"Don't get sassy with me, woman. Just run me a bath...and put some of that jasmine scented stuff in...it relaxes me."

Placing a kiss on the tip of his nose, I do as he asks. I finish running our bath, complete with a splash of lilac and jasmine bubble bath, and then we both climb in. We lie with my back to his front, surrounded by bubbles and blissfully happy.

40
KALLEN

...mid June

TODAY IS THE CHAMPIONSHIP GAME DAY AND I FEEL like a kid on Christmas morning. We'll be facing off against the San Francisco Saints, one of the few teams we've lost against this season and in the last one, it came down to a sudden death followed by a shoot-out. During which, I let the puck slip through giving them the win. I will not be letting that happen again today.

Kendall flew down a few days ago and has been staying with Chelsea and me. Chels officially moved in a few weeks ago, she was pretty much living at my place anyway, and it made sense to give up her apartment. No need to be paying rent on a place she's never at.

Grabbing my bag, I'm ready to head out when my sister walks into the living room, she's decked out head to toe in Crushers' gear. "Now, Kal," she states in her 'I mean business' tone. "You didn't fuck up my team and you're playing for the Cup but you better bring the Cup home or I'm holding you personally responsible."

"You do realize that it's a team sport, right, Kendall?"

"You remind me of that constantly and, dear Baby Bro, I don't care," she nonchalantly says with a shrug. "If the Crushers lose, it will be all your fault and I'm going to unfamily you."

"No pressure and FYI, unfamily isn't a word."

"It's all right, babe, I'll be your family." Chelsea offers me the support that I should be getting from my sister. Walking over to her, I pull her into my arms, dip her backward, and slam my lips to hers.

Kendall fake gags from beside us. "Gross, Mom and Dad are kissing."

"You're such a dork," I throw at her when I place Chelsea back on her feet. "Now, I have to go. See you ladies after we win."

"That's the spirit," my sister cheers and walks toward me. "And good luck out there tonight, Baby Bro. I'm so proud of you." She pulls me in for a hug, holding on a little tighter and without uttering any words, I know she's feeling what I'm feeling. Not having Nanna and Pops here is a sucker punch to the gut. I need to win today, for them...and for my big sister.

Walking through the players' entrance, I'm on a high like I've never felt before. It's always great to make the finals but to be playing for The Cup, it's a dream come true AND in my rookie year to boot.

Of course, the first person I see is Doucheman. After the incident a few months back, we came to an agreement, of sorts. He would leave us alone and try not to be a douche. For the most part he hasn't been a douche, but the douche in Däuchmen is hard to keep away.

Rumor has it, Däuchmen will be playing for the LA Legends next season, or so Doucheman is saying. He's been nonstop bragging they're going to make him an offer he can't refuse once free agency opens up. He becomes a free agent after tonight's game and then he's free to leave. Hell, I'll hold the door open for him and give him a send-off.

I'm pulling on the last of my gear when Anton walks in. Everyone starts cheering and clapping for our captain. He's grinning like a mofo because not only is it Cup day but it's also his last game ever. He announced his retirement last week so a win for him today would be extra great.

"It's game day, boys," he croons. Walking around the room, tapping everyone affectionately on the head—with a not so affectionate tap for Doucheman.

We can hear the rumbles from the crowd echo down the tunnel toward us in the locker room and it adds to the already electric atmosphere. I have a good feeling about today. Nanna and Pops are up there watching over me and the team.

"Wanna make a bet?" JJ asks, clapping me on the back.

"I was wondering if you'd want to place one today."

"I'm always up for it."

"Up for losing again?" I tease him. I can't remember the last time I lost one of these. "What you got in mind?"

"Why do I have to come up with it?"

"Loser's choice," I reply with a shrug.

"Isn't it usually winner's choice?"

"Well, I was going to give you a go since you never get a chance to set them since you've lost the last..." He flips me the bird. "You need to have an assist percentage higher than eight-six for the game." JJ is weird and likes to calculate his percentages and try and increase it each game. It's kind of a brilliant way to track your skill level but don't tell him I said that.

"What's yours?"

"Maximum of one goal for the Saints tonight."

"What's at stake?"

"Loser has to shave his head for the entire off-season and grow a mustache. Style may change throughout but you must always have a stash."

"Deal."

We each spit on our palms and shake. "You're going down, Jones," JJ says.

"I highly doubt it, Jameson," I cockily reply using his first name rather than his nickname.

Coach walks in and we all cheer. He hushes us and then gives his usual before game speech. With his speech over, he looks over the team and then says the magic words, "It's game time, boys, make me proud."

Wow, what a game. The final score, 3-2, in our favor. A goal from Anton, with a textbook assist from JJ, sealed the win for us in the last seconds of the game. We are all jumping and hugging each other. Slapping one another on the back. The crowd cheering and going wild, it's the best feeling in the entire pucking world.

...three days later

We're at some fancy schmancy restaurant for our team celebration but personally, I'd rather still be celebrating one-on-one with Chelsea...naked.

Sitting here waiting for her to arrive, I'm nervous because I have to tell her that I have to shave my head and grow a mustache. Hopefully she likes creepy-looking guys.

"Looks like your luscious locks are goneski." JJ claps me on the back, handing me a beer.

"You could still be up for a shave too; you haven't calculated your percentage yet." Bringing the bottle to my lips, I take a sip, a half the bottle is now empty sip, to try and calm my nerves. I've never been so nervous in my life.

"Duuuuude, I was on fire in that game, there's no fucking way I'm shaving."

"We'll see, but I will say, that assist at the end there was everything."

"I know, right?" he replies and it's not in his usual

cocky way. "I'm so glad that Anton is going out on a high."

"Yeah, me too." Then I feel her, without turning around, I know she's here. Looking over my shoulder, I grin when I see her, the last few hours without her while she and her mom were at the salon has been hell. "Excuse me," I tell JJ and before he can reply, I stand up. I need to see my girl.

"Pussy-whipped," he fake coughs. Flipping him the bird behind my back, I make my way over to Chels. As soon as she sees me, a megawatt smile graces her face.

"How does it feel to be a winner?" she asks me, throwing her arms around my neck. She's asked this question relentlessly since we won three days ago.

"Great, because I have you."

She rolls her eyes at me. "You're lucky I love you and your cheesiness."

"That's not all you love." Before she can reply, I slam my lips to her and kiss the life out of her. My tongue plunges into her mouth for a searing X-rated kiss.

"Get a room, you two," JJ shouts from behind me. Again, I flip him the bird and continue to kiss my girlfriend. We stand here in the middle of the room kissing. I don't register anyone else around us.

Breaking the kiss, I take her hand in mine and pull her to head back to where I was with JJ, but when I turn back around, he's chatting with Lexi. Not wanting to interrupt, I change course and head to the bar to grab Chels a glass of wine and another beer for me.

"Should we get tequila?" I whisper into her ear as we wait for our drinks.

"There's already a bottle waiting for us at home."

"I knew I loved you for a reason."

The bartender clears his throat, nodding to our drinks. "Thanks, man."

Picking up our drinks, Chels raises hers up. "Congrats on winning the Cup in your rookie season."

"I'll drink to that," I reply, tapping my bottle to her glass. Bringing the bottle to my lips, I take a sip. "I'm still in shock that we won. When I let that puck through and we were tied, I was sure it was going to end in a sudden death."

"I think everyone did."

"But then Anton and JJ, fuck, that goal was phenomenal." I'm still in shock over that shot.

"For a few seconds the entire place went silent because everyone was holding their breath. Their eyes locked on the puck but once recognition hit that it went in..." She shakes her head side to side. "I've never seen a crowd go wild like they did."

Pulling her into my arms, I stare down at her. "I think we should get out of here and celebrate the win, just the two of us...again."

"Ohh, I plan on doing that but first, we need to be team players and celebrate here." She leans into me, her warm breath hits my skin and she huskily whispers, "I may also have a sexy cheerleader outfit to aid in our celebration tonight." She pulls back and winks at me.

"Sure we can't leave now?"

"I'm sure. Now, let's go celebrate with the rest of the Cup winners."

"How did I get so lucky to snag a gal like you?"

She shrugs her shoulders at me and smiles. Turning away from me, she walks over to her mom and dad. She sways her hips side to side and all I'm picturing right now is her in a sexy as fuck cheerleader outfit riding my cock.

I really am a lucky son of a bitch. I, well my team, won the Cup and my girlfriend is the best girlfriend in the history of girlfriends. Life could not get any better than this.

EPILOGUE - KALLEN

...twelve months later

"And the winner of the Stanley Cup for the second year in a row, the New York Crushers."

The arena erupts into cheers. Jett, our new captain, walks over and accepts the Cup from Melton Oliver. He'll be punching a chubbie right now because Oliver is his idol and the reason he became a player.

Once everything wraps up, we head out and celebrate, and just like last year, three days later, we do the traditional end of season team dinner with all the Crushers staff and family.

JJ bumps shoulders with me, a large grin on his face, a grin that I'm pretty sure mirrors mine right now. We kept our tradition of dares going but this year, he dared me to propose to Chelsea tonight... if we won. It was a dare that

I was willing to take because regardless of if we won or not, I was asking her.

A few weeks ago, I invited them both to lunch to ask Coach and Nessa's permission to marry their daughter...

...I'm sitting in the diner where we had brunch the morning after Chelsea and I officially got together. Coach and Nessa should be here any minute and I'm shitting bricks right now. I'm more nervous than when I was waiting for the drafts to be announced.

My leg bounces up and down and I'm biting my thumbnail. The longer I wait the more I think that Coach is going to kick my ass for even suggesting I marry Chelsea, and he'll have me doing bag skates for the rest of my life.

"Sorry we're late," Nessa says, sliding into the booth across from me. "There was an accident and then we couldn't find an open garage."

"It's fine," I tell her.

"You okay, Jones? You look like you're ready to blow chunks."

"David," Nessa berates her husband, slapping him on the arm.

The waitress arrives and we all order our coffees. As she walks away, I take a deep breath, about to give my speech when Nessa looks to her husband. "You remember what it was like when you went and asked my dad to marry me? You ne—"

"You know I'm going to ask permission?" I interrupt.

"That fact you invited us to coffee without Chels was kind of a giveaway."

"Ohh," I state and to reiterate the coffee without Chelsea, the waitress returns with our drinks. Picking mine up, I take a sip and scald my mouth on the hot liquid.

Closing my eyes, I take another deep breath, trying to calm my nerves. Looking over at them, I go to open my mouth but Nessa beats me to it. "Yes, yes, you can," Nessa says, smiling across at me. "I couldn't think of a better person for our daughter."

Coach groans and I begin to think he's not on board with this.

"Play nice, David," Nessa snaps at her husband, then, with one sentence, she becomes my most favorite person in the world, well, apart from her daughter that is. "Just be thankful it's not Stefan sitting across from us asking for our daughter's hand in marriage."

"I would have flat-out refused to let him marry my Pumpkin," Coach growls. He looks across the table at me. His stare is intense. "Jones, you better look after my baby. I have a gun and I'm not afraid to use it."

Nodding, I swallow deeply. "Understood, Coach, but I don't plan on ever hurting her. Your daughter is the best thing to ever happen to me and I'm not going to do anything to mess that up."

"Good," he matter-of-factly states. He looks to Nessa. "Come on, Nessa, let's leave our future son-in-law alone."

With that, he and Nessa leave the diner, and me with the bill, but I'll pay the bill for the rest of my life if it means he'd give me permission to marry Chels. Now, I just need to figure out how to do it and keep it a secret...

...After my trip down memory lane, I'm ready. I'm ready to do this.

"Come with me," I demand. Pulling on her hand, we head to the exit. Nodding at Coach and Nessa on our way out, he grins and nods and Nessa, well, she's smiling and already has tears in her eyes.

Walking to the private dining room next to ours, I put my palm on the handle, take a deep breath and open the door. Stepping aside, I let Chels go in first. She gasps when she takes in the scene before her.

The small room is filled with tealight candles and vases of Casa Blanca lilies, her favorite flower. "Kal, what...what is all this?" she asks, spinning to face me.

When she turns around, I'm down on bended knee with Nanna's engagement ring in my hands. "Chels, you came into my life when I thought I had everything I ever wanted, but when I met you, I knew you were the final piece to my everything. You tried to push me away but I'm a persistent puckhead and I wasn't going anywhere, not without you anyway. I want forever with you so, Chelsea Maxwell, will you marry me?"

"Yes. Yes. Yes. A thousand times yes. I'll marry you, Kallen Jones."

Slipping Nanna's ring onto her finger, I gaze down at her hand and can't help but smile. I know that Nanna and Pops are looking down on me, smiling and happy for me. For us. Chels lifts her hand to look at it, then she grips my cheeks, leans forward, and kisses me. Our first kiss as an engaged couple is perfect.

She pulls back and rests her forehead against mine. "I

don't pucking hate that I love you, Kallen Jones. I'm going to pucking love you 'til the end of time."

"Puck yeah, you are and for the record, I fucking love you to the end of the Earth and back and I cannot wait to make you my wife."

...a few months later

"I now pronounce you husband and wife. You may kiss the bride."

"Finally." I grip my wife's cheeks in my palms and I press my lips to hers. Our first kiss as husband and wife is perfect in every way.

We decided that we couldn't wait to get married. So, with the assistance of my sister and her friend, Bryce, we arranged an intimate ceremony at Rockwater Secret Cove in Halfmoon Bay, about two and a half hours north of Vancouver, before the start of the following season. Bryce and her husband eloped here a few years ago. As soon as we pulled up, I knew it was the place that I wanted to make Chels my wife.

My life is now complete. I'm one of the top goalies in the NHL and today, today I married my best friend. I cannot wait to grow old with her by my side and one day see her stomach grow with our child.

"I love you, wife."

"I pucking love you, husband, now come here and kiss me."

"With pleasure." Dipping her backward, I kiss my wife like my life depends on it, and I will continue to kiss her whenever she wants for the rest of my life.

EPILOGUE - CHELSEA

...seven years later

"I PUCKING HATE YOU, KALLEN JONES," I SCREAM AS another contraction hits. Baby Jones number five is making his entry into the world, joining his four sisters at home. I'm so glad this one is a boy because poor Kal needs a testosterone increase at home. I feel sorry for him and Bean, because the girls will all be going through puberty at the same time I'll be going through menopause —fun times are ahead in the Jones household.

"Okay, Chelsea, on the next contraction I need you to push."

"I can't," I cry. "I can't do this." I've been in labor for thirty-two hours now and I'm exhausted, I just want to sleep.

"Yes you can, babe. You've done this before," Kal tries to placate me but right now, the sound of his voice makes me want to punch him in his beautiful face. This is all his fault, after the twins, we agreed that he was going to have a vasectomy but would you believe it, I got pregnant while breastfeeding when the girls were three months old and three days before Kal went in for the snip.

So our dream family of three children: two girls and a boy—is now five, four girls and one boy—and I know as soon as they put my baby in my arms I will love him with all my heart. And once again, Kal, but seriously, he is NEVER coming near my vagina again. Knowing my luck, that tube they sliced when he had his vasectomy will have reattached and his super sperm will once again impregnate me and I'll be preggers with baby Jones number six.

"Never again," I screech, just as the contraction hits. Squeezing Kal's hand, I close my eyes, clench my teeth, and push with everything that I have.

"Great work, Chels," the doctor says from between my legs. "I can see the head, one more push and your lil' boy will be here."

Nodding, I take a deep breath and when the contraction hits, I push and push, and then a little cry echoes around the delivery suite. Kal cuts the cord and then our lil' man is whisked off for his checks. Once he's given the all-clear, Kal carries him over to me and places him onto my chest.

Wrapping my arms gently around him, I stare down at my beautiful baby boy. "Hi, baby," I coo, "I'm your mommy." Kissing his head, I close my eyes and breathe in that new baby scent.

Looking up at Kal with tears in my eyes, I smile at my husband and baby daddy. "Kal, he's perfect."

"He sure is, but then again, you are his mom."

"Kaaaaal," I cry, "stop being so sweet when I was a raging bitch, wishing your death, five minutes ago."

"To be fair, you were pushing a human being out of your vagina. That gives you the right to say anything you want. There's no way in hell I could do that. Like seriously, if having babies was left to us men, Earth would be unpopulated very quickly. I'd rather take a puck to the head."

I laugh at his words. "I pucking love you."

"I pucking love you too. Now, I'm going to get the girls from Grandpa and Nanny so they can meet their baby brother." He gently runs his fingertip over our lil' man's cheek and then kisses my temple.

"Wait," I shout, "he needs a name, and I think I want to call him Matthew, after your pops."

"It's perfect." Kal leans down and presses his lips to mine. "Back soon, Matty Moo." He kisses Matthew's head and walks out of my hospital room. Soaking up the quiet, I enjoy it while I can because when Mom and Dad arrive with the girls, it's going to be chaotic.

A knock on the door startles me, I'd drifted off to sleep with Mathew suckling at my boob. Clearly, he's a boob man like his dad because he latched on with no worries, completely different from his sisters. "Come in," I whisper-shout.

Dad pokes his head in, and I expect Mom, the girls, and Kal to follow but it's just him. "Hey, Pumpkin, how you feeling?"

"Exhausted but this lil' guy here makes it all worth it." He walks in, quietly closing the door behind him. "Dad, I'd like you to meet Matthew David Jones." I haven't run his middle name by Kal yet, but I'm sure he'll be okay with it.

Dad's eyes widen when he realizes that we gave him his middle name. "Is his middle name after me?"

Nodding, I smile at him. "Yep, his first name is after Kal's Pops."

Before we can talk further, the door opens and in comes Mom holding Martha's hand as she pushes the stroller with a sleeping Elle and Callie. Behind them, Kal has Kaylee in his arms. And can I say, there is nothing hotter than a dad holding his daughter in his arms...and that right there is why we have five kids. My husband is hotter than puck.

Matthew is quickly whipped out of my arms. Mom and the girls showering him in kisses, and Dad watches over them with a goofy proud grin on his face.

Kal walks over to me and climbs onto the bed next to me, pulling me into his side. "Howz it goin'?"

"I'm exhausted but at the same time energized...and wondering how in the puck I'm going to do this." Looking over this time, I tell him exactly what's on my mind. "How the puck am I going to do this? Five kids under six, what the puck?"

"We'll get through it, Chels, and I will be there every step of the way. You and me, we're a team and Team Jones is the best pucking team around."

My heart soars at hearing him say that and if I hadn't just pushed his nine-pound son out of my hoo-ha, I'd be mounting him. "And you saying things like that is why we have five kids, but thank puck you've had the snip because if you keep being swoony like that, I'm sure we'd have enough kids to start our own hockey team."

"I'm never going to stop making you quiver with desire like that, Mrs. Jones. And for the record, I'd love to make a hockey team with you, but I'm also happy to stop at five. Just an FYI, I could be a bus driver and pull out to avoid children."

"We all know you're good at avoiding buses, but I think I'd rather rely on medical intervention for that. Plus, you ain't gonna deny me an orgasm just to avoid kids. It's all or nothing, baby."

"Fair enough." He places his finger under my chin and directs my head toward him. He leans down and kisses me. Closing my eyes, I give myself over to Kallen and the kiss.

I'm the luckiest woman in the world. I have a husband who loves me unconditionally. Five amazing children and an extended family who would do anything for one another. I'm the pucking luckiest woman in the world and I'm so glad I gave him a chance.

The Pucking End!

Want to know more about Kallen's big sister Kendall? Grab Seven Kisses now and see if she gets her HEA like her baby brother.

It was only meant to be a New Year's kiss for Huxley and Kendall, but one kiss wasn't enough.
Seven kisses was all it took for them to know they'd found their happily ever after.
It seemed simple enough, but fate kept pulling them apart.
They hoped to have forever, but they were about to find out, happily ever afters might only be for fairy tales.

One kiss just wasn't enough

ACKNOWLEDGMENTS

These things never get any easier and after 26 books (thanks Karen for pointing that out to me) this one has been hard to write.

Karen Hrdlicka from **Barren Acres Editing**; thank you for everything that you do for me.

Lisa and **Margaret;** thank you for checking all my I's are dotted, my T's are crossed and there's no extra e's or s's....and Margaret, glad you agree that they DO hang it wrong and yes, let's not get started on the dishwasher LOL

Renae from **R.L. Cover Designs**; thank you for brining Kallen to life. This image is perfect for him and you nailed it.

Sammy from **Sammy Bee Designs**; thanks for all of the amazing teasers. You always nail it and I love working with you.

Lainey from **DS Promotions** and all of the bloggers, thank you for helping me share IPHTILY with the world.

My beta babes **Bec, Tara, Sarah, Jackie and Vi;** I would be lost without you ladies. You give me advice when I second guess everything and you helped to bring this story to life. Thank you from the bottom of my heart. Special shout out to Jackie for helping this Aussie with all the ice hockey stuff.

Troy, my husband, my everything. You really are awesome at what you do and you are an even better husband and father. Love you long-time dude.

To my munchkins, **Piper** and **Kade**. You two are my greatest achievement and I'm so lucky to have you both in my life. Love you long-time guys and I look forward to the day when you are forty and can finally read my books.

And finally, **you, my reader**. This book is a different genre for me but I have to say, its one of my favs and I hope that you loved Chelsea and Kallen as much as I do.

Cheers,
Dana XoXoX

PLAYLIST

Thunderstruck - AC/DC
Song 2 - Blur
Seven Nation Army - The White Stripes
Eye of the Tiger - Survivor
I'm Yours - Jason Mraz
Can't Fight This Feeling - REO Speedwagon
Beneath Your Beautiful - Labrinth
Good Feeling - Flo Rider
I Gotta Feeling - Back Eyed Peas
Bangarang - Skrillex feat. Sirah
Don't Stop Me Now - Queen
Open Your Eyes - Snow Patrol
You Belong With Me - Taylor Swift
Paparazzi - Lady Gaga
Breakeven - The Script
I Know You Want Me - Pitbull
Bad Liar - Imagine Dragons
Someone You Loved - Lewis Capaldi
On Top Of The World - Imagine Dragons

Bad Romance - Lady Gaga
Hall of Fame - The Script feat Will.i.am
Just Give Me a Reason - P!nk
Before He Cheats - Carrie Underwood
American Idiot - Green Day
Whistle - Flo Rida
Furious - JaRule

This playlist can be found on Spotify.

ALSO BY DL GALLIE

STAND ALONES

Antecedent

Doc Steel

Oops

Off the Books

Fractured:A driven world novel

Deck...the Balls

Secrets and Sunrises

Always in the Cards

Out of Nowhere

Before the Ashes

After the Ashes

Love Me Like You Do

Never Let Me Go

Seven Nights

Seven Kisses

PUCKING NOVELS

I Pucking Hate That I Love You

A Pucking Good Christmas

I Pucking Hate That You Love Me

...and a few pucking more

FALLING NOVELS

These men make it hard not to fall for them

Falling for Dr. Kelly

Falling for Dr. Knight

Falling for Agent Cox

Falling for Agent Cruz

Falling: The Complete Collection

LORDS OF CRESTWOOD PREP

Co-write with Tara Lee

Thatcher

Reign

Hendrix

Saint

THE UNEXPECTED SERIES

When it comes to love, expect the unexpected

The Unexpected Gift

The Unexpected Letter

The Unexpected Package

The Unexpected Connection

The Unexpected series: The Complete Collection

THE CASTAWAY GROVE COLLECTION

Love has arrived in the Grove

Oasis

Unequivocal Love

Five Words

Broken Rules

...and a few more to come.

The Castaway Grove Collection, Vol 1

THE LIQUOR CABINET SERIES

Liquor has never been so disturbingly saucy

Malt Me (Book 1)

Tequila Healing (Book 2)

Wine Not (Book 3)

The Final Shot (Book 4)

The Liquor Cabinet: Series boxset

FACEBOOK ~ INSTAGRAM ~ BOOKBUB

GOODREADS ~ WEBSITE

dlgallieauthor@outlook.com

Sign up to my newsletter

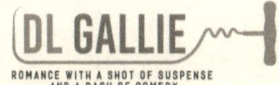

ABOUT THE AUTHOR

DL Gallie is from Queensland, Australia, but she's lived in many different places all over the world, including the UK and Canada. She currently resides in Central Queensland with her husband and two munchkins. She and her husband have been together since she was sixteen, and although they drive each other crazy at times, she couldn't imagine her life without him.

Shortly after her son was born, DL began reading again. With encouragement from her husband, she picked up the pen and started writing, and now the voices in her head won't shut up.

DL enjoys listening to music, drinking white wine in the summer, red wine in the winter, and beer all year round. She's also never been known to turn down a cocktail, especially a margarita.